Rewritten I:
Fallacy

Rewritten I:
Fallacy

Morgan Bauman

Qol Press

Portland, OR, USA

This book is a work of fiction. Any references to historical events, real people, or real locales are used fictitiously. Other names, characters, places, and incidents are the product of the author's imagination, and any resemblance to actual events or locales or persons, living or dead, is entirely coincidental.

Other Editions

ISBN 978-1-938776-00-7 (pbk.)
ISBN 978-1-938776-01-4 (.pdf)
ISBN 978-1-938776-02-1 (.mobi)
ISBN 978-1-938776-03-8 (.epub)
ISBN 978-1-938776-04-5 (audbk.)

For all those who have ever asked:

"What if?"

Table of Contents

Table of Contents (cont.)

ACKNOWLEDGMENTS

Every book, I suspect, is the culmination of years of work for many different people. Some people may contribute by lending a critical eye, while others may do so by encouraging the author to keep writing. A few—or, hopefully, many—will stand up and support the book as an audience.

In my opinion, the most meaningful support comes from those who buy the book, those who enjoy the book, and those who go on to build fan communities devoted to the book—such people may not always rally around a given book, but their existence certainly enriches the reading (and writing) experience.

This book, especially, relied on the support of others to get off of the ground. In the beginning, Natalie Luvera read my awful first draft and told me she loved it; Ashley Koenig encouraged me to rewrite the book not once but twice. My parents supported me throughout high school rewrites and vanity publishing misadventures. I have been so fortunate to have met people through the internet who gave me feedback and rooted for me when it looked like this pipe dream of mine would never come true.

Then I turned to KickStarter.

It was a month that I won't soon forget. Long nights lying awake in bed, wondering what more I could do—long days trying to come up with rewards that people would enjoy. The night before the campaign ended, the situation was bleak. I was most of the way there, but the final leap looked impossibly high.

Then I got a signal boost that sent enormous amounts of traffic my way. Backers poured in, and I hit my goal—I started crying on the phone, half delirious, not sure that I wasn't dreaming. (Although I don't think that one can hyperventilate in dreams.) I had never experienced such overwhelming gratitude; my heart was so full that it took me several hours to find any words at all.

To my backers: you have irrevocably changed my life. I don't care how large or small your donation was—your support has made me abundantly and enormously happy. I want to take this space to thank you personally. *(I would also like to thank those that are unnamed; they just preferred not to be listed below. All names are listed alphabetically by first name if provided.)*

Adam L. Zink,

Annemiek Hamelink,

B.S.,

Brian White,

Connie Chinn,

Corvus,

Dan 'stuffe' Wilkinson,

David Low,

Deb Richardson,

Desmond Kidney,

Elisabeth Kilcrease,

Erin Lee,

Felipe Foltran,

Francesca,

Heather Swanston,

Heather Ewert,

Jennifer Davis,

Jessica Walker,

Jessie Myers,

JJ Oxford,

J.P. Doherty,

Kage Davies,

Keith Hall,

Lee R Tracy

Maggie Korenblium,

Mike Skolnik,

Nadia Cerezo,

N. M. Carrara,

Paul Haggerty,

Peter Davis,

Rachel Anne,

Rhel ná DecVandé,

Sarah Bouwsma,

Shyam Nunley,

StewartN,

Valentina Centurelli,

Mr. Wook,

and, finally, I would never have made it this far without The Voice of Ra—also known as Zeus, God of Thunder. Well, you know, that one guy—you know the one. His support has been invaluable throughout the writing, editing, and publication of this tome.

I would also like to thank the artists and editors who made this book possible. Thank you, first of all, to Gail Lynn Sapitan, who drew both the cover and the scenery concept art. Thank you also to Susan Lau, who illustrated the character profiles and interaction scenes. Thank you, Jeff Miller, for the 3D model of the Haubonalyr. Thank you to Tamara and Katinka Thorondor for the action scene's illustration. Thank you also to Herwin Wielink for the maps. To my editors—Hildred Billings, Oksana Bondar, Natalie Luvera, Agnes Nogal, and Rico—your comments and feedback have been absolutely critical to the development of this book. Thank you.

Last but not least, I want to thank my best friend. She has supported me through every draft, every life change, and every moment of despair. I would not be the person I am today without her. To Ashley Koenig, *thank you*. Thank you so much for everything.

- Morgan Bauman

INTRODUCTION

Fantasy can hold up a mirror and show us what our monsters are, masking them in the safety of improbable distance. Fantasy can challenge our assumptions and subvert our expectations. Fantasy can appear to be one thing in order to convince us to consider another; it's an inkblot onto which we project what we think we see.

The world of Qol is entirely fictitious, but I tried to give it firm enough foundations to make it a realistic fantasy. Those who have read advance copies of the book have come to me with a number of interpretations about that world and how it relates to our own. I do not intend to spoil everyone's fun by clearly stating at the outset what I meant to say with these books. When it comes right down to it, what I meant to say is irrelevant. The joy of a book is forming a personal connection with it, imbuing it with your own meaning and opinions.

I wrote this series because I believed it was a story worth writing. I am publishing it now because others have told me that it is also a story worth reading. I will leave that for you to decide.

- Morgan Bauman

mbauman@qolpress.com

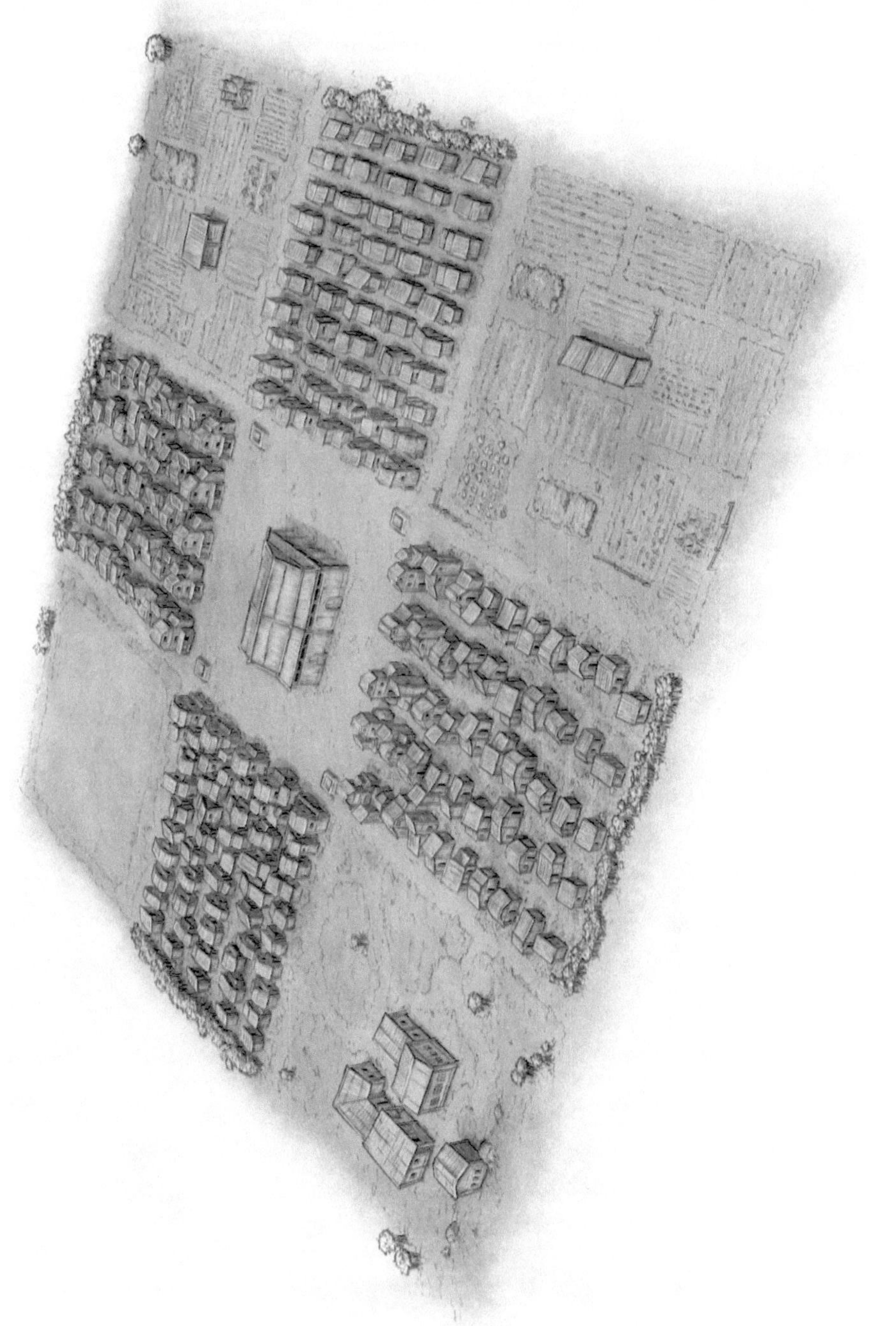

CHAPTER ONE

Laenyn's feet felt like stones; they dragged beneath her, unwilling to carry her where she intended to go. She kept her head high and her stride strong, even though her heart pounded in her chest, begging her to live, to go back to her daughter, to go back to the misery that was life as a Keshaan.

Wylwon opened her mouth to speak, but no words came out. Instead, she looked back, making sure no one watched them walk into the Kahro forest. It was so early in the morning that there was barely a hint of golden light on the horizon, but Laenyn felt the White eyes on her as she went to visit the only woman to ever live outside the bounds of the village.

The path was well kept, as it led to the lake as well as to Jauge's house. Jauge didn't fit; the Council had thought it safest to grant her request to live with her daughter, alone in the woods.

Laenyn's heart ached.

"Mother?" Laenyn asked, her voice hoarse. Wylwon looked up, her hair slipping free of its ponytail. Her hair looked gray with age in the darkness. Laenyn swallowed and looked away. "The waxed cloth will make a good water skin."

"The light that she's promised me would be more helpful

right now," Wylwon said, a trace of a sigh in her voice. Laenyn's feet refused to move faster, despite the pain and grief. Wylwon fell silent, and the silence lapsed—the sky was patterned with a bronze canopy and a deep, purple sky, with only the barest touch of daylight beyond it all. Laenyn watched that sky and wished that she'd held her daughter more tightly before she'd left.

Eventually, the trees thinned, and they turned to the left to enter Jauge's clearing. Jauge's house was entirely unlike the staunch, uniformly cut buildings of Ilonon. The door swung in and out rather than sliding quietly and elegantly to the side, smoke curled upward from a square stack that rose from the roof, and light reflected on the windows as the moons moved overhead.

Laenyn looked up at the moons, staring longest at the gray moon. Her lips moved silently as she prayed: *Please, give my daughter a better mother. And, I beg you, let me sleep.*

Breathing out slowly to disguise her sigh, Laenyn left her mother at the porch and rapped once at the post beside the doorway.

"Come in." Jauge's voice was unforgettable—a caustic growl that sneered no matter what expression she wore. Laenyn closed her eyes, steeled herself, and walked through the door. Jauge was ready, a crooked half-smile on her face, the chair prepared. "You're a little early," she remarked. Laenyn nodded, her voice failing her. The feet that had brought her this far seemed to abandon her, and she swayed suddenly. Jauge caught her by the shoulder, the slitted pupils of her White eyes flashing gold in the firelight.

"Forgive me," Laenyn said, then wished she could take back the words. Pain flashed across Jauge's face before she could put up the smile again. The silence burned in the air; too many words left unsaid, too many accusations stifled. Laenyn could barely breathe. Jauge's gaze stung. Her eyes were too much like—no. Laenyn swallowed, willing her body to remember her training, fighting to do as she had always done and follow orders.

Sick to her stomach, Laenyn allowed herself to be led to the chair, let the devices be strapped to her head, let Jauge undo the braid that was the symbol of everything she had tried to achieve.

"Are you certain that you will go through with it?" Jauge murmured, her white hair clinging to her sweaty forehead, stark against her dark skin. The room was chilly, and the wires on Laenyn's forehead clung to her like a spiderweb.

"Yes," Laenyn replied, though her body screamed *No!* Her spirit flagged and quailed beneath the towering grief. Jauge chuckled, her throat dry and raspy.

"There will be no coming back, you know," Jauge pressed.

"I know," Laenyn whispered. The straps were cold and her arms were losing circulation; it felt like relief.

"Good girl, good," Jauge said. She had a lopsided slash of a smile, and her eyes were too bright and feverish. Laenyn's body knew fear; Laenyn's heart sang for release. "Now, dear, just close your eyes and relax. It will all be over soon."

Renee Marie Marsh
(Ray)

CHAPTER TWO

Ray's eyes snapped open. The woman's sharp grin burned in her mind's eye for a moment before fading. Ray leapt out of bed, throwing off her blanket. Her bedroom was the same as ever: sun-bleached, neat, and impersonal. Something was off—but as she turned to hunt down exactly what was wrong, it seemed to skirt the edge of her vision. Everything was in order: her computer on a desk at the foot of her bed, her dressers against the wall, the dusty mirrors on her closet door, showing her as a somewhat scrawny 10-year-old with brown hair and green eyes, wearing pajamas that were much too big for her.

What was out of place? She shook her head. The door to her right was full of sunshine, while the door to her left led to the rest of the house. Ray swallowed, but she was parched. She padded down the hall, hardly aware of the floor beneath her feet.

Her mother was in the kitchen. Ray avoided her gaze, turning to sit at the table. A heap of pancakes awaited her. The thought of choking food down her dry throat made her want to gag.

"Eat up, honey," Ray's mom said, with an empty cheer in her voice. Ray didn't bother to ask; she knew what was wrong. There was water in the fridge, beyond her mother—Ray licked her cracked lips and turned away. Sitting at the table, Ray forced down her pancakes in silence and let her mother go back to cook-ing, which was what occupied her time when she wanted a dis-traction. When Ray's father got upset, he would leave the house. He wasn't around much these days.

"Mom?" Ray said, when she'd finished eating. Her mother turned and looked in her direction, but didn't quite meet her eyes.

"Did you want to go swimming, sweetie?" her mother asked. Ray couldn't remember what she'd wanted, or whether she'd wanted anything at all. She nodded. "Go ask Meg. Haven is in the pool right now. Meg should be watching her."

Hearing her mother's voice hurt; she sounded lifeless and hollow. Ray stood, opening her mouth to speak, but her mother looked back to the sink, turning a clean dish over and over in her hands. When Ray examined at her, all she could see was her hair, colorless and faded. It might have once been brown or blonde, but Ray couldn't recall. Swallowing her thought, Ray turned and left.

It seemed much later in the day than Ray had first thought. The sun was high in the sky; heat steamed off the ground and made the air hazy. Phoenix burned in the summer. The grass was a washed out yellow, dried and dead—only the pool shone blue and colorful beneath the oppressive sun, smooth as a looking glass.

Meg stood by the pool. She had friends over; Ray never learned the names of Meg's friends, no matter how often they came by. The haze made them blur together. Only Meg was clear-ly defined. Ray could hear the murmur of their voices, and the dim impression of laughter, but she ignored them for the mo-ment. She set her eyes on Haven instead. Haven paddled in the shallow end, though Ray knew Haven was a good swimmer for a five-year-old. Seeing her made Ray burn on the inside—it was a fury that was outside her, beyond her. The brat swam on, oblivi-ous. Her face shone through the heat haze, youthful and freckled.

Her red curls were brown when wet and glistened in the blistering sunlight.

Ray's tongue was thick in her mouth, and her skin was so dry it seemed to crack and peel. Only Meg could let her into the pool. She walked toward Meg, who was looking out at Haven. The beautifully pristine, blue sky glowed above Meg's head. Ray's eyes were cloudy with sleepiness again; they unfocused, and Meg's face blurred.

"I want to swim, Meg," Ray said, her voice dry, her throat parched. Meg continued talking, and Ray focused on her words.

"I know that it wasn't my fault, but I can't help feeling as though, you know, it was. Like I should have done something. Or known, at least."

The sound of a passing car drowned out her friend's voice as she replied, and Meg sighed.

"But she won't let go—I don't know what to do. I thought she was safe from her, but even now, after all these years... It's hard to be your sister's keeper."

Ray stiffened. Frustration tore at her, smoldering in her chest —the rage and loathing that had surrounded her when she first saw Haven came back to her, overwhelming her. She just wanted to swim. Why was everything always about that brat?

One of Meg's friends seemed to have been speaking, though her words might as well have been the sighing of the wind. As Meg spoke, Ray felt dizzy and desperate for water.

"It's not right," Meg said, "Ray is still— You don't understand."

"Understand what, Meg?" Ray asked, fighting to speak around her swollen tongue. Meg spun and gasped.

"Ray!" Meg said. "How long have you been standing there?"

Ray ignored her. The sun beat down on her; it was imperative that she dive into the pool. Her head rang with a headache so sharp and hot that she thought, for a moment, that she'd have to cut a hole in her skull and let water rush in to ease the burn.

"Let me swim, Meg."

"Haven's swimming right now," Meg replied, a hint of fear in her eyes. The undertone that lurked beneath her words was bright and sore in Ray's mind.

"Well, I want to swim, too!" Ray said, voice sharp and too loud. Meg took a step back, and her friends parted behind her like water.

"I can't let you—" Meg began, then swallowed, "I can't let you go in unsupervised."

"Fine," Ray said, "After you, then."

Meg looked startled, then glanced around at her friends. They seemed to shrug, and Ray realized that Meg was already in her swimsuit. Though she couldn't remember when she'd put it on, Ray looked down and saw herself in a swimsuit of her own. She looked up and found herself by the diving board.

With nothing more than a sideways glance at Ray, Meg climbed onto the diving board. She leapt into the pool, and the splash stung Ray's eyes. She rubbed them, feeling almost as though she was stirring in her sleep. By the time they were clear again, Meg was out of the pool, looking mournfully at Haven and dangling her feet in the water. Was it guilt or helplessness in her expression? Ray understood—and yet drew back from the understanding.

"Good luck, honey!" their mother called from the doorway. Ray glanced at her, but the glare on the door was too bright; she couldn't see her. Instead, Ray turned her attention to her feet.

Ray hopped up to the diving board, bouncing with each step. The water sparkled in the sunshine. She took a deep breath, did a simple dive, and slipped through the water, eyes shut tight against the chlorine. Pausing underwater for a moment to enjoy how cold the water was, she kicked off and soared upward toward the world above.

CHAPTER THREE

Ray burst out of the water, gasping for air—it was frigid and burned in her lungs. Ray's eyes flew open, and she choked as bitter water got in her mouth. A woman on the shore spun to look at her, but Ray ignored her. The pool was gone. She felt for an end to the water, but there was nothing at all for her to stand on. As the wind picked up, Ray shuddered and ducked under the water that had felt so cold only moments ago, taking refuge in its warmth.

"Laenyn!" the woman on the shore shouted. "Ettyl e chy sen za kival? Arrmetlida!"

Ray shook her head, scanning the black lake that stretched out around her. Everything felt sharp and too clear. The sky was clouded over, but green peeked out between the clouds. Ray forgot to breathe, forgot to paddle, and a little swell splashed into her mouth, making her gasp and breaking the spell. The woman was still shouting—in the moments before Ray's attention snapped back to her, it sounded like she was being scolded for going into the cold, for not asking permission, for—Ray looked at the woman and found that the words made no sense.

"Carremaen!" the woman was shouting, her hair coming loose from her ponytail as she waved her arms above her head.

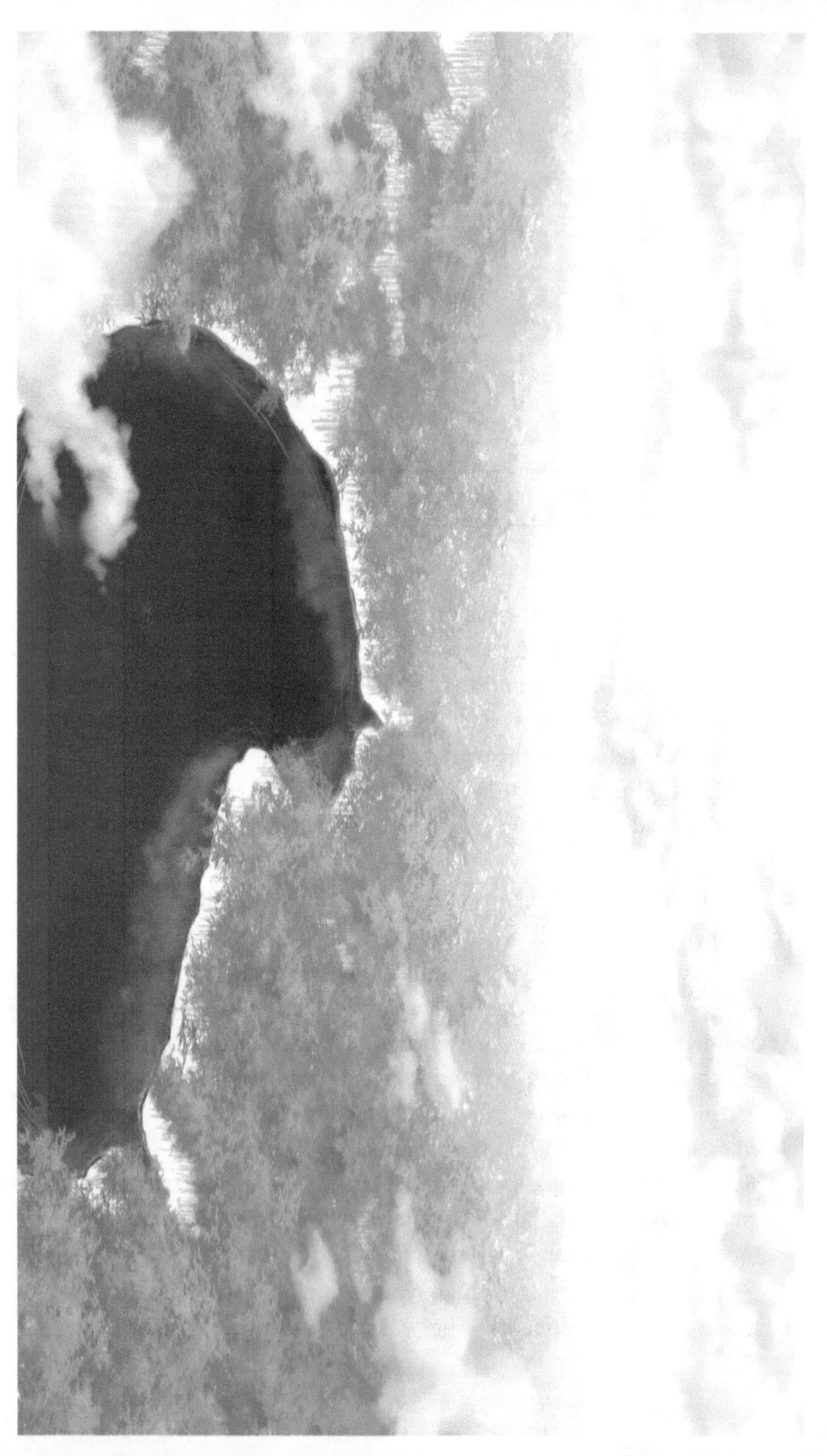

"Ettyl e chy sen za kival? Asah—arrmetlida!"

Ray swam toward her, though her hands shook and her hair chilled the skin where it clung plastered to her face. There was no one around; her family was gone, her anger fizzling as icy fear drenched her. On the shore, white stalks thin enough to grip with one hand stood close together. High above them hung a bronze-colored canopy, uniting the trunks into a single forest. The air smelled of flowers.

These little details overwhelmed her—the cracks that ran like spiderwebs over the bark, the rustle of a small animal in the thick brush, the metallic taste of the water, the soft, tickling brush of seaweed against her foot, the scent of lilacs and lavender and things she'd never thought of before. There were no sounds like cars honking and Meg's friends murmuring; there was no sun with its enormous, oppressive heat; and the world felt much, much wider.

Pulling herself out of the water with the exceptionally soft, red grass that should have torn under her grip and didn't, Ray curled up on the shore and closed her eyes. There was no way to close her ears, though, or her nose. All familiar things were absent here. Her heart split in her chest with someone else's pain until her own panic surged over it, drowning out the mournful cry with a scream of terror.

"Laenyn!" the woman said, shaking Ray by the shoulder. The touch was too solid, too real; Ray could feel the cracks in her hands, the pressure and discomfort of a hand squeezing her. "Ettel e chy tynithina?" The woman's voice was breaking. "Tyff toqu y terrempata?" Ray looked up at the woman's horrified tone.

"What's wrong?" Ray heard herself ask. She watched the woman's expression shift until tears pooled in the woman's eyes. Ray was at a loss—she couldn't think of what to say, or how to get the woman to understand her. Nothing was right in the world. Nothing made sense. "I—maybe I can help?" Ray asked, her voice sounding like someone else's, adding to the feeling of vertigo that seemed ready to knock her into the sky.

"No, no," the woman said. Tears were in her eyes, and Ray noticed that they were a dull brown. Even though the woman was dry, and Ray was soaking wet, the woman dragged her into a hug, burying her face in Ray's shoulder. "No, no, it was not to work! It was not to work!"

Ray shoved her away and scrambled backward, trying to get to her feet. Her limbs were all wrong: they were gangly and wild, and she fell to the ground, getting her long, green dress tangled around her ankles. The grass was slick with translucent, turquoise-colored water, lending a purple sheen to it. Details seemed to overpower her, keeping her from seeing the whole picture, but suddenly it came together, breaking through the sickening nausea of displacement.

"Where am I?" Ray asked, trying not to realize that there was no way for her pool to link to this lake, no way for summer to become autumn in a moment's time underwater. "Who are you?"

"Mother," the woman sobbed, pointing to herself. "Daughter," she said, grabbing Ray for another hug. "My daughter, my daughter."

"You're not my mother!" Ray said, trying to pry herself from the woman's embrace, but her grip was unrelenting. "I don't know who you are!"

"Wylwon Laenyn Emmerven," the woman said. "My name with yours. Oh, Laenyn."

"Let me go," Ray insisted. The woman drew back.

"I am Wylwon," the woman said. Ray pulled away from her, looking around at the lake, with its smooth, black water. "This is entirely my fault. Oh, stars," Ray looked back at Wylwon, and she continued in the other language, "Y toqu bevvenpata nu raishet chy, en toh chy sara raishet y. Kywonnh—"

"Wait, how did your English get better all of a sudden?" Ray asked. Wylwon stopped mid-sentence, staring at Ray.

"Y e lyassapata Yra," she replied, tentatively reaching out to touch Ray's face. When Ray grimaced and pulled away, agony flooded her expression. "Why only English?"

"I'm not your daughter," Ray insisted. "I don't speak your language. I don't know where I am!"

"Haven knows English," Wylwon said.

"Haven?" Ray repeated. Not a common name—not easy to mistake. Maybe she wasn't far from home. Even though anyone would've been better than the brat, Ray needed to find her way home. Haven would know how she'd gotten here.

"Yes," Wylwon said. "Your daughter."

Ray's head ached—too much to take in, and none of it piecing together. She looked up at the sky, which was turning blue overhead, but it was the wrong blue. It was off; it was alien and unsettling. It was a point between dark green and deep, royal purple, a color she'd never known before, a color she couldn't recognize. She heard Wylwon curse and mutter about fog, but she couldn't repeat the words that she'd used.

"We have to go," Wylwon said, looking into Ray's eyes. Tears cut lines through the dust on her cheeks, but she smudged them away.

"I'm not going anywhere with you!" Ray said, her voice too deep and developed. It made her sound twice her age. She felt like crying, herself. "What's going on? I want to go home!"

"Home?" Wylwon repeated. Ray nodded furiously. "I can take you home."

Ray looked around. The lake was at least a mile wide, and the trees seemed towering at twenty feet. Phoenix didn't have trees, not ones that belonged there. Swallowing, Ray shook her head.

"That's impossible," she whispered. "This isn't real. None of this is real."

"Please, Laenyn!" Wylwon said, lapsing back into the other language as Ray looked at her. "Tohn toqu kyt kevven. Tohn toqu nu fah. Za shevvek e fen, sy yo e inech carremaen."

"I can't understand you!" Ray said. "Where's home? I want to go home."

"I can take you home," Wylwon said, running a hand over her hair to smooth back her ponytail. "I can take you home. Follow."

Wylwon gestured for Ray to follow, but once Ray had struggled to her feet, she hesitated. There was no one around, but was that a good reason to go with a stranger? It was dizzying to look down at Wylwon and the ground; she was too tall, too tall!

"Please!" Wylwon begged, looking over at the lake. Ray followed her gaze and realized that a thick, blue smog was beginning to froth at the surface, rising as the sky got darker. It seemed to glow in the twilit air, and it grew higher and thicker with every moment. Wylwon's eyes were wild, and she grabbed Ray's hand. "Please follow!" she said. Ray stared back at the smog, which spread out over the lake's surface, moving slowly but inexorably outward, getting ever thicker as it traveled.

"What is that?" Ray felt herself ask. There was a ringing in her ears, an acrid scent on the breeze.

"Dangerous!" Wylwon said. Her voice was high with fright. "No touch! No breathe! Follow!"

Ray saw a large water skimmer drift by on the lake; as the fog enveloped it, it spasmed, and white film coated its eyes as black veins sprung up along its skin, which cracked.

It sank.

"Yeah," Ray said, backing up. The sound of a frog's panicked croaking died. "Yeah, I'll follow you. Let's go! Let's go!"

They ran toward a hole in the trees, and Ray's feet found the path before she could see it; everything before her was made dim and indistinct by the canopy above and her own shadow as she was lit from behind by the fog, which lent a slight, sickly glow to the world. Ray saw ghastly faces in the trees' webbed bark, but she and the stranger ran past them, onto a path that couldn't possibly take her home.

CHAPTER FOUR

The trees weren't quite trees—they swayed, pliable, in the moonlight, shifting at the outskirts of Ray's vision as she raced past them. Tangled in their midst were scarred, inflexible trees with roots that knotted around Ray's feet as she fled. The impenetrable wall of wood and undergrowth confined them to a narrow, unkempt path. The woman ahead of her seemed to know almost instinctively where to leap over roots, where to skirt past rogue branches, how to evade the forest's clutches. Ray's too-long limbs caught on rough bark that splintered, biting into her skin.

The woman vanished into the darkness ahead, where the path curved, her footsteps dampened by the layer of slick, dead leaves on the ground. Ray collapsed, winded.

"What am I doing here?" she asked herself. The forest seemed to creak around her; mist settled on her face, cold as sweat after a nightmare. Shuddering, Ray curled in on herself. "I want to go home. Where am I supposed to go from here? Where the hell am I?" The word felt grown-up on her lips, and she blushed in the darkness. Opening her eyes, Ray let out a slow breath and pushed herself to her feet. Her legs felt long and ungainly as she peered into the woods.

The forest seemed cluttered at the edges; shadows darted in

and out of sight as the moonlight shifted and the branches swayed in a breeze that was beyond Ray's reach.

"Look," Ray said, her mouth dry, "I'm not scared of anything!" Her voice shook just enough to give away her lie. She swallowed again. "I'm not! I'm not afraid of anything in the whole world!" A bird took flight in the tree above her, making Ray shrink back against the tree. Ray licked her lips. "I'm going to find a way home, okay? I'll do it all on my own."

The path went only two ways; toward death at the lake, and toward the terrifying, unknown place to which Wylwon had fled. Taking in a deep breath that smelled something like honeysuckle and something like lemongrass, Ray went down the path that the woman had followed.

"I'm not going to get lost," Ray announced. Her footfalls were too heavy, too loud; her heart pounded in her chest. "It's safe as long as I'm on the path!"

A twig snapped as something darted through the underbrush; Ray caught a glimpse of a tiny, black shape running through the shadows. A wave of nauseating fear swept through her as another, larger animal gave chase. In the underbrush, something squealed, and she could hear lips and fangs smacking. Her feet began to run without her realizing it, and she almost stumbled and fell as she spun around to watch an owl ghost through the canopy above her, letting out a loud hoot that made Ray shriek and duck as she covered her hair.

"I'm not scared!" Ray shouted, trying to anchor herself. Her breaths came in gasps, but she forced herself to slow down and breathe normally. "I'm just looking for my home, okay? So you'd better leave me alone, or you'll be sorry!"

The path was long and dark, and Ray had nothing to light her way. The animals that leapt deeper into the forest at her approach scared her at first, but as she got her bearings, she began to growl and shout at them. Each cry sent them further into the woods, until, finally, Ray was left in silence, with only her footsteps to remind her that she hadn't gone deaf, and that she was still moving forward. Not even bugs rattled and sang in the dark reaches of the woods.

How had she gotten here? Ray didn't want to think about it, but the question lurked at the edges of her consciousness, making her uneasy. There was no explanation for it—unless her pool had a hole that led to that lake, there was no way to make sense of it. Ray shivered, longing for the bright sunlight that had driven her into the water in the first place. Her hair and dress were still dripping, and even the slightest breeze made her shake like the last autumn leaf clinging to a tree.

Just then, a dim, blue glow fell on the ground before her, though the trees cut deep holes in the light. The light swayed, and Ray made out another shadow on the forest floor: a person holding out an arm, reaching into the night. Ray froze, afraid to make any sound at all. Had Wylwon come back to help her? Ray didn't know what Wylwon wanted from her.

But the woman that emerged from around the bend was much older than Wylwon. Her hair was a stark white and cropped close to her face. The woman's eyes glinted in the blue light, shining like a cat's. Ray held her breath, wishing that she could become invisible.

The woman looked at her with a crooked half-smile, and Ray let out her breath.

"Hello there, Ray," the woman said. Her voice was raspy; Ray guessed that she was a heavy smoker. "I understand that you got lost in the woods."

"How do you know who I am?" Ray asked, willing her voice not to tremble. "Who told you where I was?"

"Your mother is worried about you," the woman laughed; it sounded like the barking of a dog.

"You know where my mother is?" Ray demanded, hope surging in her chest. The woman held out her hand.

"I even know where Phoenix is," she said. "Come over to my

Jauge Haunobolon Kahn

house. I think that we need to talk."

"Who are you?" Ray asked, though she stepped forward and reached, hesitantly, for the woman's hand. "What's going on?"

"All in good time, my dear," she said, smiling again. Ray realized that the woman stood a good foot shorter than she did. "My name is Jauge. Jauge Haunobolon Kahn. Now, come this way."

Ray's hand dropped to her side, but she followed Jauge through the night.

"How do you know English?" Ray asked. "Wylwon didn't know English. Where am I?"

Jauge said nothing, but held up the pale, blue lantern and padded, silent as a cat, down the path. Ray felt as though she knew Jauge from somewhere—from something like a dream. A chill crawled down her spine, but she suppressed the shudder. The path opened to their right, and Ray saw a house lit with a dozen little lanterns.

"Welcome," Jauge said, hopping nimbly up the steps. Ray's legs wobbled beneath her, but she followed Jauge through the door and into the house. There was a couch, a love seat, and a chair circled around a low coffee table—all made of wood that had been painted white. There were padded cushions on them. The wall ahead of her was filled with books from floor to ceiling, though they weren't bound. To her left was a taller table covered in papers and surrounded by incomprehensible machines, as well as an assortment of potted plants. The wall to her right was covered with large strips of paper that had complicated diagrams drawn in painstaking detail.

Jauge coughed, and Ray looked down at her. Jauge's eyes were golden, with cat's pupils.

"Contacts?" Ray asked. Jauge laughed, her pupils shrinking as they adjusted to the bright light in the room.

"Have a seat," Jauge said, motioning to the chair. Ray went toward it, then, feeling unnerved, sat down on the couch beside it. Jauge sat on the love seat across from her, resting her chin on her hands as she examined Ray.

"I really should get going soon," Ray said, unable to look away from Jauge's gaze. "You said that Mom was worried about me."

"Yes, your mother is quite concerned," Jauge said, frowning a little. She flung a piece of charcoal at Ray. "Catch."

Ray caught it, even though she nearly missed. It left black smudges on her hands.

"Motor reflexes seem to be functional," Jauge muttered. Ray set the charcoal down on the table, watching as her fingers left smudges that were a deep green rather than black. "Look up," Jauge said sharply. Ray obeyed, trying to dust her hands off. Jauge held up a string with a stone tied at the end. "Watch this, but don't turn your head."

"What are you doing?" Ray demanded, getting to her feet. Jauge set down the string and grinned.

"You hit your head rather badly, I'm afraid," she said. Ray was good at spotting a liar—something about the way Jauge's eyes dilated, the way she looked away, told her that Jauge wasn't being honest with her. "When you dove into the water, I think that you struck your head on a rock. Didn't you come to with a headache?"

"Yes," Ray said, feeling her head for lumps until Jauge looked at her again. Her gaze seemed to cut through Ray; she dropped her hand at once. "But what's it to you? Who are you?"

"Call me a friend," Jauge said. "I see that you've forgotten some things."

"How did I get here?" Ray demanded. "Don't tell me that I've got amnesia—I don't! I can remember everything just fine!"

"Fine then," Jauge said, standing with a shrug. "If you re-member everything, then there's no need for me to explain any-thing. You ought to run on home, then. Good night, Ray."

"Wait!" Ray said, holding her hand out and clenching it into a fist as Jauge walked away from her. "Wait, wait. Okay, so I don't remember how I got here. I don't remember how to get home."

"You're much calmer than I anticipated," Jauge sighed, glancing at Ray sidelong. "I'd thought... But never mind what I thought. Take the path to Ilonon if you want to find your home; Haven has all the answers."

"Haven?" Ray repeated. "The brat? What's she doing here?"

"She's awfully close-lipped on the matter," Jauge said, moving to straighten the books on the shelf. "You left a water mark on my couch, Ray."

Ray turned and looked; she'd left an entire puddle. By the time she looked up again, Jauge was waving her hand, dismissing Ray's apology before she'd even opened her mouth.

"It's no matter," Jauge said. "It's time that I sew a new one, in any case. Haven lives with Wylwon. It's too much trouble to explain it all to you—"

"But you said that we had to talk!" Ray said. Jauge's smile made anger flare in her chest.

"That's more like it," she murmured. Clearing her throat, she continued in a louder tone. "And we really did need to talk. I needed to be sure you were...in control of yourself. Now that I see you're all right, I have no further need to inquire of you. You may go."

"Go?" Ray repeated. She glanced at the door, at the dark night that waited beyond the single pane of wood. "But I—"

"No matter," Jauge said, turning away again. "I have other tasks at hand. I'm finished with you; there's no further need to concern myself. Follow the path to the right, and you'll be just fine."

"This doesn't make any sense!" Ray shouted. Jauge paused mid-gesture, reaching for a book on the highest shelf. Her arms had faint marks on them, but Ray couldn't make sense of them. "Who are you? Who's Wylwon? What's Haven doing here?" Ray punched the bookshelf as she came around Jauge's side to stare down at her. Jauge's expression was serene and pleased as Ray confronted her; Ray gritted her teeth. "You have to answer my questions! I know that you're hiding something from me!"

"I owe you nothing, Ray," Jauge said, Ray's name rolling on Jauge's tongue. Ray drew back a step. "I owe you absolutely nothing. I owe Wylwon nothing, as well. The contract has been broken; you weren't to be taken to the lake, and here you are, dripping puddles on my hardwood floors and couch." Jauge grinned, and Ray wanted to throttle her. The urge scared her, and she looked away to calm herself down.

"Stop trying to make me mad," Ray muttered. Jauge's grin vanished.

"That's all you're meant to be," Jauge said. Ray fought back the fury that rose in her chest at Jauge's condescending tone. "You don't know what you're looking for, Ray. You don't know what your home is. What questions would get you there?"

"My home is in Phoenix," Ray said.

"And Phoenix is hot, isn't it?" Jauge said. "The sky burns you?"

"My home is in Phoenix," Ray said, more fiercely.

"Odd, then, that you should find yourself in a forest in late autumn," Jauge continued. "Odd that you should recognize me, when I've never seen a desert in my life."

"My home is in Phoenix!"

"Ask a question, then," Jauge said. Ray thought back to the lake, trying to remember the point where the pool and lake had merged, the point at which she'd slipped out of the world she knew—her head rang with pain, and she sagged against the bookcase.

"Do you know?" Ray asked. She kneaded her knuckles against her forehead, trying to push back the pain. Jauge's eyes focused on her, the cat-like pupils widening to consume all but a sliver of the bronze that surrounded them.

"Haven is the one who knows what became of Phoenix."

"And what do *you* know?"

Jauge's eyes narrowed, pupils shrinking as she drew back.

"I know why you are here," Jauge said, looking away. "Erihs sy kyrr. Srena sy shur." She fixed her eyes on Ray once again. "By existing, you serve your principle purpose. By thinking, you serve a goal beyond yourself. But I owe you nothing, Ray—no one owes you answers. Answer them for yourself."

"I want to go home," Ray said, her headache receding slightly as the topic shifted.

"If you have no further questions, I suggest you take the path to the right." Jauge turned away, waving a dismissive hand at her. "Mind the monsters."

"There's no such thing," Ray snapped, then bit her tongue. "Give me a flashlight or something, at least."

"There's no such thing," Jauge repeated, then chuckled. "I did promise Wylwon a lantern. Perhaps I owe her that much."

She laughed again, throwing her head back, and Ray stumbled backwards, nearly upending a side table. Tears appeared in the wrinkles around Jauge's eyes.

"Oh, that's rich." Jauge managed to bring herself under control as Ray got to the other side of the couch. Jauge fixed Ray with her gaze, and Ray froze. "No, Ray. If you make it back to Ilonon, you can ask Haven what you're doing here. I think it would be better to learn about where you are. Memories never hold anything but grief."

Ray looked at the ground, unable to look Jauge in the eye any more. Guilt seemed to gnaw at her chest for the briefest instant—it was immediately replaced with bewilderment.

"Whatever," Ray said. She glared at the ground and swallowed, steeling herself. "I'll just go, then. You're a crazy old woman with no heart."

"None," Jauge whispered. Ray walked to the doorway, breathing out slowly to ease the knot of heated tension in her stomach. Jauge raised her voice as Ray pulled open the door. "I'll be checking up on you."

CHAPTER FIVE

Ray moved through the darkness, effecting a false confidence as she went, but she felt out of sorts. The canopy seemed thicker away from Jauge's house, and the pitch blackness made her hypervigilant to the unfamiliar sounds in the forest. Fighting back the urge to race down the path whenever she heard a twig snap wasn't doing any favors to her heart. Her head ached, and, even though she'd gotten used to her unsteady legs, she felt a lingering sense of vertigo.

How had she met Jauge? Ray had recognized that half-smile —it was something from a dream, or maybe a nightmare. The breeze picked up, and Ray trembled. Haven was waiting for her in Ilonon, whatever Ilonon was supposed to be. Of all the people that could have been there, why did it have to be the brat that Ray had to turn to?

Everything was slipping away from her in the darkness. Her mother's face looked like a ghost's, without substance or defined features. All she could see of Meg were her sad, green eyes. Her father was a silhouette in the doorway, keys in his hand, the scent of a perfume that made her gag clinging to his faded coat. What color was her mother's hair? Did Meg smell like chlorine from all her time in the pool? What did her father's voice sound like?

Ray clutched her head, breathing hard as she slowed from a run. The cracked bark looked like hideous, screaming faces, and, for an instant, the shadows looked like blood on her hands. Closing her eyes, Ray tried to imagine Haven. Red curls and brilliant, green eyes always reddened by tears. Cheeks dusted with freckles, and the smell of soap and clean cotton; a voice that stammered and caught when she was nervous. It was all there in her mind: Haven was clear when the others were muddy. Fury and frustration bit at Ray's emotions.

"Why am I so mad at her?" Ray whispered, staring through her fingers at the pale, silvery soil. She knew there was a reason, even though it eluded her the harder she sought it. Ray shook her head, which rang with pain. The path was dark, and her stomach growled with hunger, making her jump. Pushing it all aside, Ray continued down the path.

It could have been hours; it could have been minutes. There was no way to mark the time or the endless trees, which stood so thick and tall that Ray wondered whether she could leave the path even if she wanted to try it. It got denser and denser as Ray went forward, until the narrow trunks stood only a hand's width apart, barely visible through the tightly knitted canopy, which blocked out almost all light.

At long last, moonlight glistened on the dirt ahead, and the trees opened. Ray let out a breath that she hadn't known she was holding, but it caught in her throat. She felt eyes on her, watching her as she walked into the village. Shuddering, Ray looked around. The houses stood in neat lines, each identical to the other. With each progressive ring, the houses got taller, wider, and more elaborate, but it was the outermost ring that drew her attention. Faces clustered in the windows, their eyes turned directly on Ray. Each head had white hair, even the little children that could barely look over the sill.

Ray stared them down, and they vanished into the dark

depths of the houses. Not a single house was lit as far as the eye could see. Ray glanced back at the windows, and saw the faces disappear again, flitting away at the edge of her vision. The isolation was profound, and Ray suddenly missed Wylwon, who had at least wanted her to follow. Nowhere felt safe.

Taking carefully measured breaths, Ray looked up to examine the clouds. Three moons hung in the purple sky. One was just a circle of black, but another was a bright gray that looked like the dusty soil beneath her feet, and the final moon was a shockingly pure white that shone like a beacon in the sky. All the clouds that she'd seen at the lake were long gone. The sky was spotless. There was nothing to make her mistake the three moons—nothing to explain it away. Ray bit her tongue and looked at the ground, not ready to think about it. Her eyes were clouded with exhaustion, as though she'd been up since dawn, and her dress was crusty and heavy from the water.

"Where do I go?" Ray whispered. She couldn't bring herself to walk past the unblinking eyes that examined her on all sides; she couldn't bear to go back into the forest, with the shapes that darted in and out of sight, and the distant howls of predators that had caught their prey. There had been coyotes in Phoenix, but their calls hadn't been half as mournful, hadn't been half as eerie as these creatures that ran out of sight in the underbrush. Even the cat-like eyes that watched her in the pool of moonlight weren't as unsettling.

Ray found herself shaking when she looked around again. Clear, straight roads stretched for rows and rows of buildings. Ray looked at the outermost ring—five houses in a row. To her left, where the row stopped, stood a slightly larger building, austere and intimidating. To her right was a field lined with neat rows of plants, each bearing fruit or vegetables that glinted in the moonlight. The only way that looked at all promising was onward, past the watching eyes. Ray swallowed and took a step forward, noting that the faces withdrew at her approach.

As she went, she counted the rows that she passed. One: the

watchers dropped out of sight. Two: no windows to let her get even a glimpse of the inhabitants. Three: A little glow appeared behind a paper screen, only to be quickly put out. Four: Haven's face watched her from a crack in the doorway to her left.

Before Ray could do more than whip around to get a better look, Haven launched herself at her. Ray took a step backward, but Haven's arms closed around her, pulling her into an embrace so tight that it left Ray breathless. The little brat was smaller than Ray remembered, though there was something older about her face.

"Why are you—?" Ray began, but Haven shook her head. Something in Ray gave way to relief—it was like something that she saw, rather than felt. But then, so suddenly it stunned her, Ray felt rage boil upward at the sight of Haven's red curls. The rage was as abstract and detached from her as the relief had been —Ray didn't know which emotion was actually her own.

"Come this way, Mommy," Haven whispered, tugging her toward the house to their left. Ray went, though something in her tried to make her drag her feet. Ray felt splintered; none of her emotions fit or made sense. Her head ached so badly that it made her vision distort; it felt like her right eye had a mind of its own, and she couldn't get the two to work in tandem long enough to focus on anything.

The door made a slight scratching and creaking sound as Haven slid it open enough to admit Ray, though Ray could barely see it. Her head sang with grief and pain and things that couldn't fit—things that made no sense. She heard Haven's voice as though through water, too distorted to comprehend, and then Ray sank. She didn't feel the floor rise up to meet her.

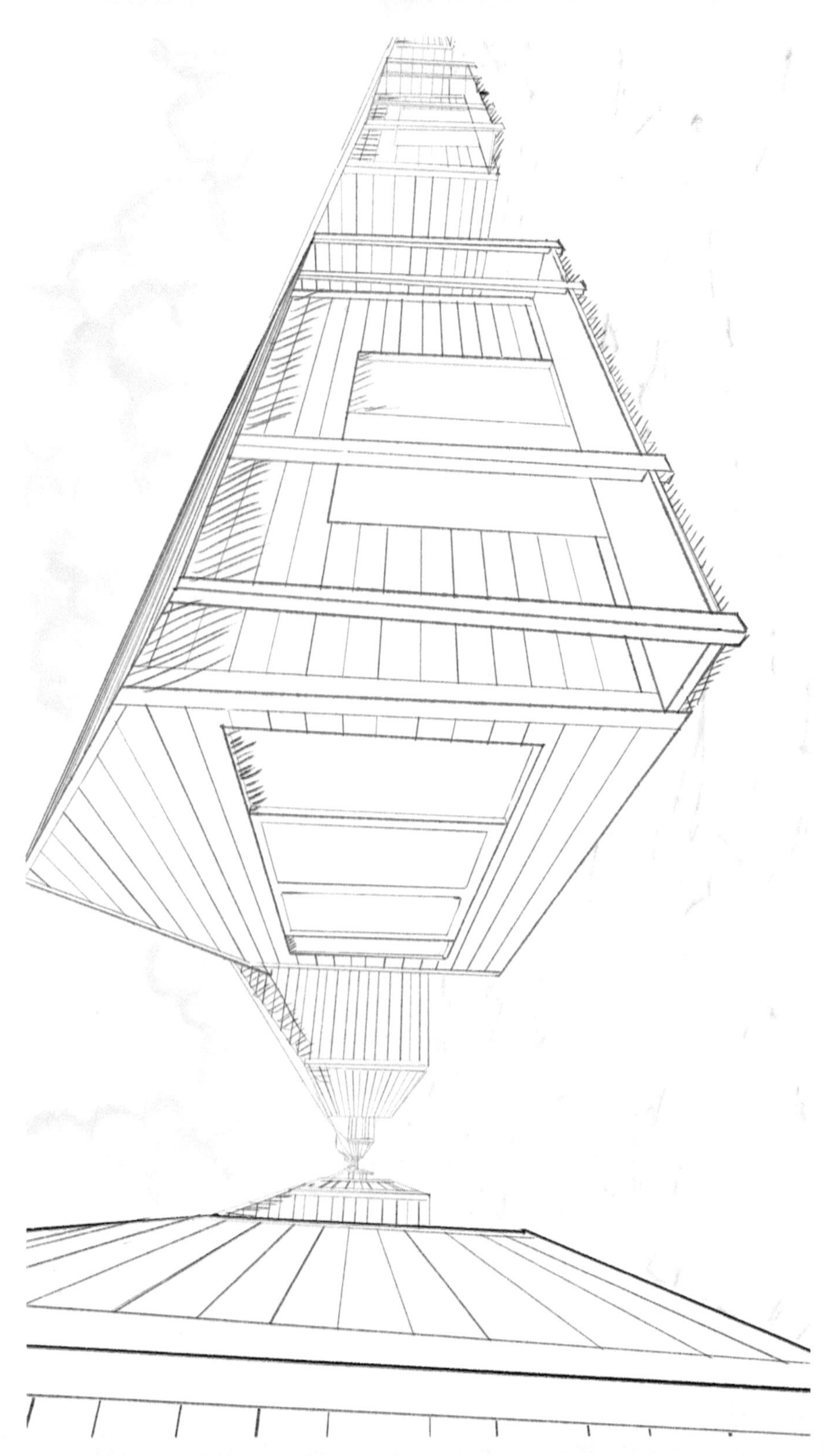

CHAPTER SIX

Golden light filled the room when Ray next opened her eyes. Blinking to blot out its brightness, Ray sat bolt upright. Haven jumped. Her hair was shorter than it had been when Ray had last seen her. The tightly wound curls poofed out when her hair was cut too short.

"Mommy!" Haven said, grinning at her. She was already sitting up, carefully tying a ribbon around her own neck. "It's time to go to breakfast now. Are you feeling all right?"

"I'm not your mother," Ray said, forcing her mouth not to snap. There was no reason to be so angry! She looked at the ground and willed herself to calm down. "I'm your sister."

"What?" Haven asked, her voice little more than a breath. Ray was surprised by the sudden tension in the air, and she looked up at Haven's horrified face. "Wylwon said that you were acting kinda strange, but..."

"I'm Ray," Ray said. "Why does everyone keep telling me that you're my daughter? What am I doing here?"

"Jauge," Haven said, and she recoiled, eyes wide. Ray put her head in her hands—Haven never got angry.

"Nothing makes sense," she whispered. "Everything is—muddled. Why am I so mad at you, Haven?"

"You've always hated me, Ray," Haven whispered. "Ever since the moment I was born. I don't want you here!" Haven's tone was sharp enough that Ray looked up at her. "Get out of Mommy! Leave me alone! Leave me alone!"

"What are you talking about, brat?" Ray demanded, unable to tamp down the frustration in her chest. "I didn't come here to get you! Hell, I don't even want to be here! If you want me to go away, tell me how to get home."

Tears pooled in Haven's eyes, and her lower lip trembled. It was a face that Ray recognized better than any, and it made her angrier still.

"You have no home!" Haven shouted, her hands clenched into fists.

"Ashya!" Wylwon called, and Haven fell silent. Ray looked over to find Wylwon's voice and saw her climbing down a ladder —there were two lofts in the house, it seemed, and neither had a railing.

"I'm n-not afraid of you any more," Haven hissed, leaning forward to look into Ray's eyes. "You're not d-doing this to me again. Let go of Mommy and quit haunting me!"

"Shut up!" Ray said, shoving Haven backward to get her out of her face. Ray breathed hard, trying to calm herself down. "I didn't even do anything!"

Haven laughed, but it sounded half-mad.

"Stop laughing at me!" Ray snapped, leaping to her feet to tower over Haven. Haven didn't stop laughing, though the laughs began to warp into sobs, and tears slipped down Haven's cheeks. Ray grabbed her by the shoulders and brought her face so close to Haven's that their noses touched. "What the hell is going on?" Ray whispered, squeezing Haven's shoulders with hands that were too big. Haven began to stifle her sobs, and Ray pulled back, looking over the edge of the loft. Wylwon was looking at her with distressed eyes. Suddenly, as Haven quieted, Ray felt the hairs on the back of her neck stand on end. She spun to look at

Haven, heart pounding, and saw that Haven's face was a mask of rage.

"I want you to l-leave right now," Haven said.

"I don't know where I am!" Ray said, her heart slowing a little. "Why are you so mad at me? I know that I teased you, but—"

"No," Haven said, looking up at her with an expression torn by grief. "No, you can't stay. I want Mommy back!"

"What are you talking about?" Ray asked, her headache pounding so loudly that it drowned out all her thoughts. It was too much—Ray didn't want to fit the pieces together. "Who's this 'Mommy' of yours? You always called Mom 'Marissa'. Where is she?"

"It's time for breakfast," Haven said. Ray snapped up to look at her, but Haven didn't meet her glare. Haven's eyes were distant. "I have to do up your braid before you go. You'll get in trouble if you go out without it."

Ray's head cleared enough to let her wonder about the braid —her hair was too short to be braided—but the pain surged again as she tried to think about her own hair. She sank to her knees and let Haven separate her hair into four bunches.

"Why would I get in trouble for having my hair loose?" Ray asked.

"Don't say a single word at breakfast," Haven said firmly. "No questions. I'll answer for you if you're asked anything. Only the Pinks would understand English, anyway."

"Pinks?" Ray repeated. Haven tugged her hair into place, making Ray wince.

"Keep your eyes off the ground and off their faces," Haven continued, tying a string around the base of the braid. "Mommy is Green, and Ilonon takes its Colors very seriously. We're not full citizens here. The Secondaries eat after the Primaries, answer to the Primaries, and do exactly as they're told. Don't object to anything, no matter what you see."

"What?" Ray asked. Her headache had dulled, but Haven's

words didn't make sense. "What do you mean?"

"We can't be late," Haven finished, getting to her feet and dusting straw off of her green dress. Ray noticed that they had been sleeping on a mound of straw covered with a patched cloth. A few stray pieces had come through the roughly sewn patches; Ray began to pick them out of her dress. Haven did it more efficiently, removing them all in a few, quick swipes.

"You have to slow down," Ray said. "Give me ten minutes to get my head around this stuff! Why won't you answer—"

"You don't deserve answers," Haven muttered, walking to the ladder. "When Mommy comes back, the point will be moot."

Ray looked down at her hands, which were plainly not her own hands. They were tough with callouses, and the fingers were long. Dark green ribbons, the same color as her dress, crisscrossed up her arms.

"What are these?" Ray asked, and Haven hesitated on the ladder, biting her lip.

"Don't take those off," Haven said. The anger in her tone had grown weary. "Please, Ray. Please just do what I say and keep yourself out of trouble."

"You need to tell me what's going on," Ray insisted. "I don't understand anything. Everything makes me angry, and I don't know why."

"You were an angry person," Haven whispered. "Whenever I was around, anyway. If you remembered—history repeats itself." Haven shuddered. "Do what I say, Ray. I don't have time to explain right now."

Ray sighed, dragging herself to her feet. "Fine," she said, the fire gone out of her. "I'll keep my head down and keep quiet."

"Now come on," Haven said, hopping onto the ladder and starting to climb down. "We're going to be late, and I don't think that you want thirty switches with a wooden stick."

Haven Emmerven

CHAPTER SEVEN

The main hall had a high ceiling, and eleven rows of tables running from left to right. There were four entrances, one on each wall. The tables to the left were covered in fine china and had well-made clay cups, while the tables to the right had chipped plates and mugs with broken handles. Haven directed her to a table a little toward the right. As people filed into the room, Ray realized that they were sorting themselves according to the color of their clothes, but it was a pattern that made no sense to her. The younger girls wore bells that rang softly at their throats; anyone older than a teenager had crisscrossing ribbons much like her own.

"Look at the table," Haven whispered. Ray could barely hear her over the shuffling of feet, the creak and clatter of benches accommodating hundreds of people, but she obeyed reluctantly. Black, blue, red, yellow, gray, brown, purple, green—they were in the green rows, surrounded by other women in cotton dresses, although Ray could tell that the women further down the table, toward the far door, were wearing other fabrics. Haven kicked her, and she looked down again, running her finger across the surface of the table.

It left a green trail, exactly the same hue as her dress. Ray froze, but Haven looked up at her with stern eyes.

"Better posture," she mouthed. Ray sat upright, wincing a little at a kink in her back. "Don't make faces. No smiles, no frowns, nothing." Haven's voice was quiet, but clear. Ray fought the urge to roll her eyes, stifled a sigh, and let Haven force her hands to her side, although her eyes watched the green streak until it faded from sight.

The room gradually fell silent. Ray tried to look up, but Haven grabbed her dress. She stared at her plate and cup instead, listening intently for some sort of explanation for the silence. Her cup had a crack that ran most of the way down its side, and her plate had such a large chip missing that Ray worried it would break if she lifted it up. It was stained and sticky with something that caught the light from the high windows. Maybe juice?

The silence wasn't quite silence; there were too many people in one place for that. The little bells rang when children shifted, and the benches beneath them creaked. Some people coughed discretely. But no one in the enormous hall spoke. Women carrying baskets of fruit and pitchers of water traveled down the lines, starting with the black table and moving forward. Ray kept her eyes fixed on her plate and cup until a woman in an orange dress stopped behind her. Wylwon lifted her hand and pressed it against the table, leaving a green stain the color of a lime's peel. It was the shape of her handprint and as clear as if she'd dipped her hand in paint first. The woman tipped her head and set down what looked like a large apple that had dark, green skin.

Ray mimicked Wylwon, leaving a green handprint that was a hue darker than Wylwon's. Tipping her head again, the woman in orange set another dark green fruit down on Ray's plate. Ray opened her mouth to thank the woman, but Haven's grip on her dress tightened, and Ray closed her mouth. Another woman, this one in yellow with a haughty expression of condescension, came by to pour water into her cup. It leaked out through the crack, and the woman sneered, though she said nothing. Anger flared in Ray's chest, but Haven's hand was insistent.

The sound of eating was a low bustle in the hall; people didn't speak, but they shifted, and the fruits seemed to have a little crunch to them. Ray eyed hers warily, not sure how to go about eating it. It was larger than her too-large hands, wide enough that taking a bite seemed problematic.

"Eat," Haven whispered, taking a bite of the fruit. Ray held in a sigh and picked up the heavy fruit. It was cool to the touch; she took a bite and found that its texture was like that of an apple, though its juice was as plentiful and sweet as a pear's. It tasted better than she'd expected, though she still wished for something warm.

Ray heard the sound of ceramic shattering. She began to turn, but Haven yanked her back and tipped her arm upward. Ray ate obediently, though her ears were pricked, and it was a struggle to keep her eyes on her plate.

"Kywonnh hakkyllida, plyam essa," a woman's voice begged. Quiet though it was, it was easy to discern in the still hall. She was near tears, or worn ragged with exhaustion. Ray guessed that she was middle-aged. "Y e srenaspata. Shaal e kerren!"

"Ashya," an old woman's voice said. Ray spotted her out of the corner of her eye—she sat at the head of the table on the far side of the room, and her voice was lazy and regal. Though there was nothing menacing in her tone, a shudder ran through the crowd. The fruit tasted bitter in Ray's mouth. "Chy ny kyp erre-vanpata ky ny shaan. Tyff e chy yulln nu aren?"

There was a moment of silence. A child choked back a sob.

"Etten," the woman replied, her voice hoarse.

"Fy," the old woman chuckled. "Sych."

"Ermen?" The first woman's voice caught, and the child sobbed, whispering something that Ray couldn't make out. The rest of the people in the hall went back to eating, ignoring the scene entirely. Haven bit her lip, though, and Ray knew by their tone that something was wrong.

"Lon-om," the older woman replied, her voice suddenly

sharp. Ray went back to eating slowly as silence lapsed, but suddenly the silence was broken by a sharp crack and a child's wail. Haven dragged Ray's gaze back to her plate, but the sound came again and again—it was the sound of a slap. By the end, the child was sobbing, and Ray's hands were shaking. Somehow, the food on her plate was gone, and her fingers and lips were sticky with its juice. It tasted like bile in her throat. The room began to clear, and the footsteps of a hundred people drowned out the child's soft, hiccuping sobs.

Haven dragged her to the door, glaring at Ray when she made to turn back and look for the crying child. The crowd dispersed; those in black went to the first row of houses, those in blue to the next. Beneath her feet, the dirt felt cold through the thin soles of Ray's shoes, and the bright air felt dank on her forearms. Her ribbons clung tightly to her skin, tugging little enough that Ray could ignore them, but never so little that she could fully forget them.

"What was that about?" Ray hissed, her voice catching in her throat. She felt sick. "What happened back there?"

"Wait until we're home," Haven murmured, looking at some women in pink as they bowed ahead of her, hiding a child in their midst. "I told you to stay quiet."

Ray gritted her teeth. The sound of the little girl wailing still rang in her ears. Ray had smacked Haven a few times in the past, but Haven had never wailed like that—a headache snapped at Ray as she even considered the thought, and she pulled back.

Finally, Haven darted ahead and slid open the door, letting Wylwon and Ray through before slipping inside and shutting it behind her.

"What was that about?" Ray demanded, keeping her voice low. "Why did they beat up that kid?"

"She broke a plate," Haven said, looking away. Wylwon watched them with furrowed eyebrows, lost. "You never balked at hitting anyone who misbehaved," Haven whispered. Ray bit her tongue, fighting down her frustration.

"But that's not enough to—" Ray began. "The plates were broken to begin with!"

"The Pink family barely gets anything that's not in pieces," Haven said. She sighed. "The Yellow woman who was pouring the water knocked the girl's plate onto the ground on purpose. She's the one who broke it."

"But then why blame the kid?" Ray asked, trying to run a hand through her hair and finding her progress halted by the braid. "Smack that stupid smirk off the woman in the yellow dress!"

"It's not just a dress, Ray," Haven said, pulling a hand through her own curls. She led Ray to the right, opening a door to admit them into the space beneath the loft. It looked like a walk-in closet. Ray waited for Haven to explain, and finally Haven sighed, leaning her head back against the wall. "That woman was a pure Yellow. Completely pure. Sure, she was Cotton, too, but that's an Ilononian distinction. I told you that Ilonon takes its Colors seriously. Do you honestly believe that a Yellow woman would be blamed when a Pink child could take it for her?"

"What are you talking about?" Ray demanded, falling back against the wall and sliding down to look across at Haven. "What's with all this Color stuff? I don't know what you're saying."

"Sure you don't," Haven muttered, rolling her eyes. "Come on, we only get a few more minutes before it's time for mandatory exercise, and then you have to go off to Keshaan training. Ask me something useful."

"I honestly don't know what the hell you're talking about!" Ray snapped. "What colors? What do you mean, pure? What's this about cotton?"

"Cotton is a Ilononian way of making more distinctions between the Colors," Haven said, twirling a lock of hair around her finger. "Cotton is the lowest. Wool is above Cotton, Velvet is above Wool, and Silk is above Velvet."

"Wool? I didn't see any place for livestock," Ray said, thinking of the lack of meat and the tall rows of fruit plants.

"I call it wool, but that's just because there's no word for it in English," Haven sighed. "Same with silk. They make everything from plant fibers. I just call it that based on the texture. Come on, Ray, I'm sure that you have more important questions. I'm only going to answer one more."

"Explain these colors to me, then," Ray said, leaning back against the cool wood and closing her eyes. "What's this about purity? And why did that woman at the black table have any right to tell the woman to beat up her kid?"

"That woman was the Black Council Woman," Haven said. "I guess you wouldn't know about that, since we didn't have a Council in Phoenix. That old woman was Araya Devolair Miria Senea Thyn." Fury flashed in Ray's chest, so powerful and sudden that it scared her. It felt separate from her, like she was experiencing someone else's fury. Haven sighed, and Ray became aware of the world around her again. The wood was cold and rough against her palms, even though they were thick with callouses that weren't hers. Her breaths came with little puffs of steam, and she shivered in the cold.

Haven sat back. "I don't want to explain the Council right now," she sighed, sliding a hand over her eyes. "It's hard enough to explain it without trying to cram it into the ten minutes before mandatory exercises." She looked at Ray, her eyes serious. "Don't bother asking about the exercises. Just follow the lead of the woman in front of you, and you'll be fine. Mommy's body should know the stretches, anyway. She's done them every day since she was three years old."

"You said that I'd get one more question!" Ray said, exasperation leaking into her tone. Haven rolled her eyes.

"You asked three," Haven said. Leaning forward, she narrowed her eyes. "I told you—I'm not scared of you any more. You're not going to terrify me into doing whatever you want me to do. Mommy won't let you hurt me, I know it. If you even try, then she'll rush back to get me."

"I don't want to hurt you," Ray snapped. She tried again to run a hand through her hair and cursed when it snagged in her braid. "I just want to know what's going on!"

Haven looked at Ray warily, balancing on the balls of her feet as though she might leap away at any moment.

"You're my sister, Ray, right?" Haven murmured. Her tone was so vulnerable that Ray felt startled. Haven sounded young again, and her guard was slipping. A part of Ray geared up to strike, but the rest of her shoved it down. "What do you mean when you say that you don't want to hurt me?"

"I have no reason to hurt you," Ray said, trying to make her tone convey how earnest she felt. "I don't know where I am. I don't know what I'm doing here. Everything is all wrong, and I can't put any of the pieces together. Any time I try, my head feels like it's splitting open."

Haven was silent for a long moment. Wind rattled the paper windows that caught the light and brightened the whole house; they looked faintly green.

"We'll get in trouble if we don't exercise," Haven said quietly, getting to her feet and dusting off her dress. Ray looked up; Haven's expression was soft and pensive. Examining Ray's face, she nodded. "I'll explain after training. Just don't talk to anyone, keep your head down, and do as you're told. When you go to Keshaan training, go off on your own and pretend to meditate. That should keep you mostly out of trouble."

Ray opened her mouth to reply, but Wylwon opened the door beside her, peering in with nervous eyes. Her hair was coming free of its ponytail again, and her bottom lip was red from being bitten.

"E ko junak?" she whispered, looking at Haven, but glancing

at Ray. Her expression filled with concern as she met Ray's eyes, but she looked away quickly.

"Kyt," Haven replied. Wylwon stiffened, and Haven shook her head. "Soosh... Y kemmenina, Wylwon Es. Y by kemmenina."

"Saye ko gott?" Wylwon asked, and Haven nodded. Wylwon looked at Ray, eyebrows drawn up with regret, biting her lip again. She sighed. "Et tohn toqu nu fa."

"We have to go," Haven said. Ray pushed herself to her feet. "Just do whatever Wylwon does in front of you; we'll be in a line. Don't mess anything up, and don't talk, no matter what happens. You kept trying to look when that little girl was getting slapped. *Don't*. There's nothing you can do, and if you do anything to stop them, it's not just you who's going to pay the price."

Haven walked out the door, and after a moment, Ray went after her. Nerves knotted themselves around her stomach.

"What do you mean?" Ray asked. Haven hesitated beside the door, her hand in the notch to slide it open.

"Well, it depends on how badly you mess up," Haven said. "I didn't think you'd care if you weren't the one in danger."

"What do you mean?" Ray said again, dreading the answer. Her own voice sounded low, dangerous, and foreign to her. Haven looked at the ground, digging her fingers into the door's notch.

"Well, just don't mess up," Haven said. "If you do, well, I might not be here to answer *any* of your questions."

CHAPTER EIGHT

They had lined up in rows, with Ray behind Wylwon, and Haven behind Ray. Ray didn't dare think about the women beyond them, let alone the woman in black who stood at the center of the field. The cold air made Ray fight down shivers, and her feet sank into the thick, slimy mud, which turned green as it stuck to her ankles.

Her body knew the stretches, though. Ray had to struggle to avoid understanding why her limbs were too long, too lithe—she had to focus on stretching every single muscle. After a while, she barely had to follow Wylwon's lead; each move began to lead seamlessly into the next. It was a relief to lose herself in the motion; she was flexible and strong, and she felt that knowledge with every new muscle she tried.

"Straighten your back!" the woman in black snapped. Ray lost her place in the rhythm and almost couldn't follow Wylwon's lead. The woman in black continued in the other language, using a stern, even fierce tone.

"Kywonnh," a child pleaded. "Tohn toqu kyt Plya Es. Y toqu by y ny Meren Es— Kywonnh hakkylida ko!"

Ray tried to watch Wylwon's movements, but her feet didn't fall naturally as she bent to stretch her core, and her foot slid in the mud. She'd barely caught herself when she realized that Wyl-won was halfway through the next step. The woman in black spoke sharply, and as Ray tried to copy Wylwon's next stretch, she heard another girl sob.

"Kyt y ny Meren Es!" the girl continued. "Ko e by ket yraiqen! Y e om-hau yraiqen; kywonnh ettenlida y kavan."

Ray's back cracked as she stretched, reaching between her legs. It didn't mask the sound of a young girl gasping as a sharp, high sound split the air. It whistled and struck again, and Ray realized it was a wooden switch. Her hands shook, but she bit down on her tongue, trying to distract herself with the pain. The switch rang out three more times before it withdrew, leaving the two girls sobbing.

Ray paid careful mind to Wylwon as she stooped to the ground in a lunge, and the cotton of her dress felt rough to the touch as she dug her fingers around her leg, holding the stretch. The woman in black stalked past them, her eyes darting from face to face, the switch in her hand dripping with something white and slick—but too thin to be mud? Her eyes met Ray's, and Ray broke eye contact immediately, following Wylwon as she moved. Sweat slid down her forehead, slipping into her eyes and making them sting and blur. The strange, green sky seemed to waver, and she felt suddenly disconnected from her body.

"Haven Emmerven!" the woman in black said, her voice slicing through the cold air. Ray's hands shook, but she managed to keep her face blank. "This is no game! Only scum like a Secondary would play in the mud."

"I will behave better," Haven replied, and Ray snapped back to attention, controlling her body and fighting back tremors. Haven continued in the other language, and the woman in black looked to Wylwon, who kept moving without hesitation.

"Mek-etten, Devolair Essa," Wylwon said.

"Ermen?" the woman asked.

"Kyrat ko kemmen," Wylwon replied evenly. The woman

nodded curtly.

"Tohn so kisu." Her voice was stern and smiling.

Ray didn't dare fall out of step; Haven had been right when she'd said her body would know the stretches. When they finished, they knelt in crisp lines. Beginning with the women in black, each row stood and left in turn. As the green line rose, Ray caught Haven's eye—she looked as though she'd been crying. Half her body was caked with mud that turned green where it touched her skin, down to her bare feet, and tension knotted between her eyebrows.

"Worry about me later," she whispered. "This is where you'll have Keshaan training. Wylwon has to leave for work at Anonwe, but she'll be back by dinner. I just wish that you could understand Yra."

"I wish I could, too," Ray muttered. The women behind them were dispersing, leaving her exposed.

"After being dismissed, go over there," Haven pointed to a dip in the forest wall. "You'll find a stump. Meditate in front of it when the other women get up, and don't you dare even so much as twitch. I'll see you back at the house after that Blue woman," she pointed again, more discretely, "tells you that it's time to go home."

"How will I understand her?" Ray asked, keeping her voice low. Haven rolled her eyes.

"You were Blue, Ray," she whispered. "You should know better than anyone. I'll be waiting at home, trying to keep quiet until you get back. Just behave, okay?"

Haven turned and left. Wylwon was nowhere to be seen. Ray looked at the women who had remained in the clearing. There were more than Ray had expected, at least a dozen women in black on the side nearest the village, and then there were women in blue, red, and yellow in respective lines going toward the forest. Ray remembered the tables in the big meeting hall, and, though there weren't any women in gray or brown left in the field, Ray walked over and knelt on the red grass beside the row of yellow women, trying to keep her distance.

The women knelt at rigid attention, backs perfectly straight and faces directed unwaveringly ahead of them, where a woman in blue stood. Ray fought the urge to close her eyes and sigh. Exercising hadn't eased the tension in her muscles, and with her ankles tucked under her legs, her feet were quickly falling asleep.

GO. I HAVE NOTHING TO TEACH YOU TODAY.

The words ricocheted in her mind, shattering her skull with the reverberations. As Ray bit down her gasp, the other women bowed, pressing their foreheads against the ground, and stood. Ray quickly pressed her forehead against the ground and left for the spot that Haven had indicated, trying not to walk any faster than the other women. Would walking too fast count as messing up? Or was it better than walking too slow? Some of the women kept their heads high and regal, while others kept them low—which one should she copy? How could she possibly get herself to stride and walk humbly at the same time? And how much trouble would she be in if she was caught staring at the other women? It would be bad enough if her body behaved the way that she expected it to, but with too-long arms and legs, keeping herself at a constant pace was nearly impossible.

Finally, she slipped through the hole in the forest wall and knelt before a little stump. Glancing over her shoulder, she stood instead, wiping dead grass from her knees. The red grass was longest by the stump, where it reached in bright curls over the pale wood. The color was almost identical to Haven's hair: a stunning, fiery red. With the green sky looming overhead, Ray thought the contrast was kind of pretty.

She was slouching. Ray quickly brought her posture back to the best that she could manage, and continued staring at the stump. Some of the other women had had staffs; had she forgotten one at home? Was she supposed to practice attacking the stump? Eyeing it, she thought that no real threat could be so small, unless it was a scorpion. A staff couldn't kill a scorpion, though. Nothing could kill the most dangerous scorpions; Ray dimly recalled watching one starve to death after it snuck into the house, and her parents had found no other way to kill it.

Ray made her head snap to attention, trying not to look around as she did so. She couldn't just nod off in the middle of whatever she was supposed to be doing. But what kind of a job was meditating, anyway? Focusing inward wasn't hard.

Ray took a deep breath, trying to relax her muscles. Even though she'd just spent the better part of an hour stretching, she didn't feel tired. Despite the scanty breakfast and lack of lunch, she didn't feel hungry. Some thirst made her throat sticky, but it seemed like a familiar discomfort. Ray had to consciously control her breathing, though she had no control of her heart rate; something about the knowledge made her lungs seize up. It was something that she'd known and ignored from the moment that she'd surfaced in the lake. It was something that she didn't want to know.

Focusing inward was too easy. With nothing to distract her, she became too aware of her own body—a body that didn't fit like it ought to, legs that stood too tall, a voice that was too old and deep, slight curves for her hips that swayed when she walked. These eyes saw more clearly than the eyes she remembered, and the hair that had fallen in her face when Haven had been braiding it had looked green.

This wasn't her body.

Facing it wasn't as hard as she'd expected. The knowledge had been there all along, lurking at the fringes of her mind. Somehow, she'd ended up in the body of Wylwon's daughter, Haven's new mother. But then, what had happened to—

Ray's head burst with pain, obscuring all thought. Bells clanging and children screaming and shattering plates—fire dancing around her as blood pooled in her hand and flecked her tongue, salty and impossible to forget—the feeling of vertigo, of plummeting, of being torn apart by grief—it was almost more than Ray could bear to stifle a howl of agony as she sank to her knees, clawing at her hair and ears, hissing and frothing with the mind-numbing pain.

The sky was a shade of teal when she found herself again. Her breaths were ragged, her mouth raw. How much time had passed? Ray pushed herself to her knees and knelt before the stump, shaking hard. She didn't dare follow her earlier train of thought; fear tore at her stomach, and she felt close to vomiting. So she was in someone else's body. So what? There wasn't anything to dwell on. There was no real reason to risk that awful pain again.

Eventually, the shaking slowed to a tremble. She was meditating in earnest, trying to clear her mind of all thoughts, when she realized that the sky was a twilit blue.

IT IS TIME TO RETURN TO YOUR HOMES. The blue woman's thoughts caught Ray off guard, and she gasped. I WILL WATCH YOU AT DINNER. KEEP YOUR FAMILIES IN CHECK.

Ray didn't doubt it.

CHAPTER NINE

"I'm home," Ray said softly, nervously examining the room before her. If she'd walked into the wrong house, would they kill her outright, or would they want to make a spectacle of her? Ray sagged with relief when Haven slid open the door beneath the right loft.

"Shut the door," Haven said, chewing on her lower lip. "And remember to keep your voice down while we're inside. They'll be listening."

Ray grimaced as she shut the door, a fierce longing for Phoenix welling up in her chest. Why had Haven left? Why would she ever choose a place like Ilonon over Phoenix?

"Jauge told me that you were the one who knew what'd happened to Phoenix," Ray said, turning back to look at her. Haven recoiled, half ducking behind the door.

"Before that, I have to tell you—"

"No," Ray said, remembering the pain that'd struck her down every time she tried to put the pieces together. "This can't wait any more, Haven!"

Haven opened her mouth, but the door screeched open behind Ray, and Haven's face tightened. Ray spun. Wylwon slammed the door behind her, but her expression was full of grief, not rage.

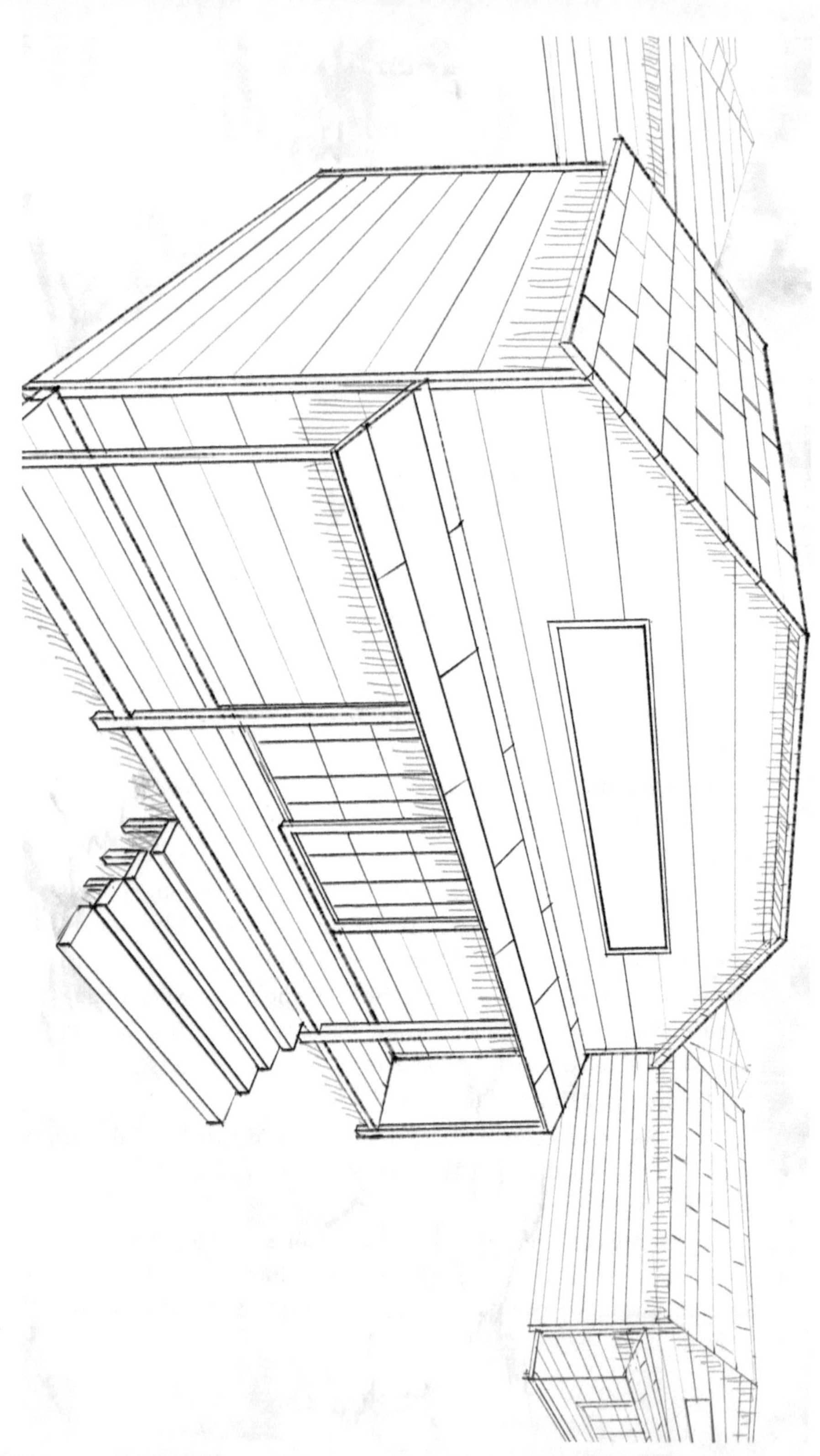

"Hakkyllida," Wylwon whispered. Haven approached her, her face serious, and Wylwon screamed. Ray flinched backward as Wylwon struck her own leg. Haven cried out as though she'd been hit, but no one stood within five feet of her. Wylwon hit her own knee again, and Haven made a high, pained noise that made Ray wince. They followed one another around the room, with Wylwon shouting and stomping as Haven sobbed and cried out. Their timing was perfect; from outside the house, it must have sounded like Wylwon was beating Haven within an inch of her life.

Ray didn't know whether to interrupt—whether she was supposed to be doing something—whether to defend Wylwon or Haven from themselves or each other. Wylwon's leg was fast becoming a mottled blue-green, but she didn't wince or hesitate until she took a moment to breathe and walked up to Haven, closing the last few feet between them.

"I'm sorry," Ray heard her whisper, but then she shouted again and struck Haven hard across the face.

Ray felt a scream rise within her, separate yet piercing: *No!*

Silence fell; the air was thick and dank as night spread beyond the window panes, and it smelled as though rain was on the verge of falling. Dust seemed to hang in the air, just visible in the last of the dying light. Ray's vision swam—Haven's gaping mouth blurred, and something hot touched her cheek. Feeling it, Ray's hand came away wet, and her vision cleared.

What just happened here?—that was the only thought that Ray could pull together through the blank wall of shock. The thought seemed to echo as though she was speaking in a vast chamber.

Haven slipped in the mud, another voice replied. A voice that she knew—it was the voice that had come out of her own mouth ever since she'd pulled herself out of that lake. Ray felt herself slip to the ground as she forgot how to control her legs.

What? It was just a thought, barely meant to be a reply. Ray's head spun.

Haven slipped in the mud, and Mother promised to beat her at home. The thoughts differed from Ray's in more than sound—they had a texture, a color, a taste, a scent—Ray pulled back, terror icy and nauseating in her stomach.

Who are you? Ray demanded, knowing already who it had to be. It felt like death had come to call, like she'd seen her own noose swaying in the wind ahead of her. She lost control of her hands, which fell limp at her side, and her eyes slipped closed.

You know, Laenyn replied.·

Ray felt overwhelmed by the sensations that erupted with each brush of Laenyn's thoughts—an overpowering scent of fresh grass, a taste so bitter that it made Ray gag, a pool so deep and viscid that she felt herself drowning—

Ray cringed and drew back from the sensations but could find no escape. Struggling through the gelatinous, jade green thoughts, unable to pull them apart and decipher them as speech, Ray fought to put up a wall between herself and Laenyn, to keep herself separate, to keep herself from being consumed alive.

What are you doing here? Ray demanded, her voice sounding as distorted as though it came through water. Everything around her disintegrated—she couldn't see beyond the words immediately before her, felt empty and turned outside in, with all of herself exposed and naked and vulnerable.

Laenyn's emotions surged like a tide over Ray, drawing her out of the soupy thought and tumbling her as a wave might, head over heels, until she lay gasping for breath.

Stop! Ray screamed. **Stop, stop!**

And it stilled.

Ray was left panting in a huddled, knotted mess, soaked to the bone. The room around her stretched on out of sight, nothing but light around her in every direction. Slowly, a floor began to materialize beneath her imagined form, and she buried her face in her hands; it didn't stop the light that scoured through her eyelids. Her eyes and throat felt raw, as though she'd been sobbing.

Slowly, she pushed herself up. A woman in a green dress sat before her. She wasn't old, though there were lines around her eyes. She had a plain face, one that would be easily forgettable if it weren't for her green hair, kept back in a thick, neat braid. Ray remembered its weight falling three or four inches past the nape of her neck. Ray noticed the drape that covered Laenyn's shoulders: the thick, coarse weave of the cloth was familiar. Laenyn's eyes were brown, much like Wylwon's; her gaze was reserved.

Forgive me, Laenyn said. Her tone was formal and distant. Ray dove, covering her head, but the tide didn't return. Embarrassed, Ray looked up at Laenyn again. *I am not used to sharing a body, let alone a mind.*

Ray nodded, not sure how to answer; her mind was blank, her mouth empty and dry.

Mother was pretending to beat Haven, Laenyn said. Ray realized that her lips weren't moving, and that the sound came from a place above and behind her ears; the visuals were imagined, but the voice felt real. *All I saw was her striking—I woke up, thinking it was a nightmare. Who are you?*

I'm Ray. Haven's older sister. Ray sat up, cross-legged—even though it was an illusion, Ray wanted to face Laenyn presentably. Ray imagined the gallows again, remembering the tide that had so nearly crushed her; Laenyn could well be her demise. With a wave of her hand, Laenyn dismissed the image.

I'm not here to kill you, Ray. Blue and white flecks appeared on the floor between them, and Ray felt guilt wash over her; it vanished in an instant, and there was grief in Laenyn's eyes. *I'm the one who shouldn't be here.*

What—?

No, forget I said anything. Laenyn looked away. The air felt heavy on Ray's shoulders, but she shook herself, trying to remember that it was all an illusion. The thoughts were real, but nothing was tangible. Laenyn sighed. *I didn't mean to come back.*

You left? Ray asked. **On purpose?**

I want to sleep, Laenyn said. Her voice sounded hollow, and Ray felt the memory of unendurable sorrow. The word sleep fell like a stone into a lake; Ray didn't want to press it. *There's nothing more to know about me.*

There's everything to know! Ray said, wincing as she found that she couldn't control what she thought aloud and what she kept to herself. **What are you?** Ray fought to bite her tongue, even clamping her hands over her mouth as the words kept pouring out. **Do you know how I got here? Why am I in your body? I can get why you'd want to leave, but why not just actually leave? Why is Haven here? How long has she been here? Why is everything color-coded? Why do they beat—**

Enough! Laenyn said, her voice snipping the thread of Ray's digression. Ray felt at a loss for words. *I have a headache. Have a little self-restraint.*

How? Ray asked, attempting to blot out the words that wanted to follow. She felt hands in her chest, throat, and brain. Before she could scream, something in her shifted, snapping into a better fit. She felt more at ease with her imagined self, and the feeling of violation disappeared in a moment. It was uncanny. Even though she wanted to feel horrified, there was a private feeling to this new state, and she felt less exposed before Laenyn's eyes. **Ah!** She had a voice, an intentional voice!

It was too hard to explain with words, and you wouldn't have understood any other way. Laenyn tilted her head slightly, examining Ray. *Now, did you really say that you don't understand the Colors?*

Everyone thinks I do, Ray said. **I have no idea what's going on.**

Jauge has some strange tricks, Laenyn said, the smile fading a little. *I don't even know where to begin. Color is in all of us. You've noticed how it draws out the pigment in the wood and soil?*

Yes.

I see that you've managed to avoid any injuries, so you might not guess this... Our blood runs true to our Color. Our sky reflects us, and the world knows us for what we are. Color is everything.

Everything, huh? Ray drawled. Laenyn's eyes snapped up to meet hers, affronted.

We have unique abilities, each according to our Color, Laenyn said, her voice shaking only a bit. *Greens, for instance, heal faster and live longer than other Colors. Aside from Black, of course.*

That doesn't seem like much, Ray replied, but she remembered the feeling of the woman in blue's thoughts. **Even then, everyone's got different talents and interests. It doesn't have to all come from your Color, does it?**

The Black family can transform their bodies, Laenyn said, her voice high and imperious. *They can become any creature of their choosing. The Purple family can make things levitate with a single thought! Those traits come from Color alone. There is no way to teach that.*

And you think that means that some abilities are better than others? Ray asked, thinking of the water-bearer and the little girl. **If there's a plague, it'd be better to be Green than Purple, wouldn't it? And if you're trying to get yourself out from under a rock or something, it'd be better to be Purple.**

Laenyn's face was stony. Ray hesitated, nervousness tingling in her stomach. She stood and walked around Laenyn. After one complete circuit, it was apparent that Laenyn had dropped the illusion. Afraid that she'd crossed some sort of line, Ray dropped the illusion, too. She settled into the part of the mind that linked up to the eyes and looked around. She saw Haven mouthing words at her; there was a shiny, blue bruise across her upper cheek.

"Haven?" Ray heard herself ask. Rain pattered on the roof, and Haven had wrapped herself up in a cloak, covering her misshapen dress. Ray felt herself sit up and her head turned, examining the fading, blue light beyond the window paper.

"We're going to be late for dinner," Haven insisted, tugging on their arm. "Are you okay?"

Hell if I know.

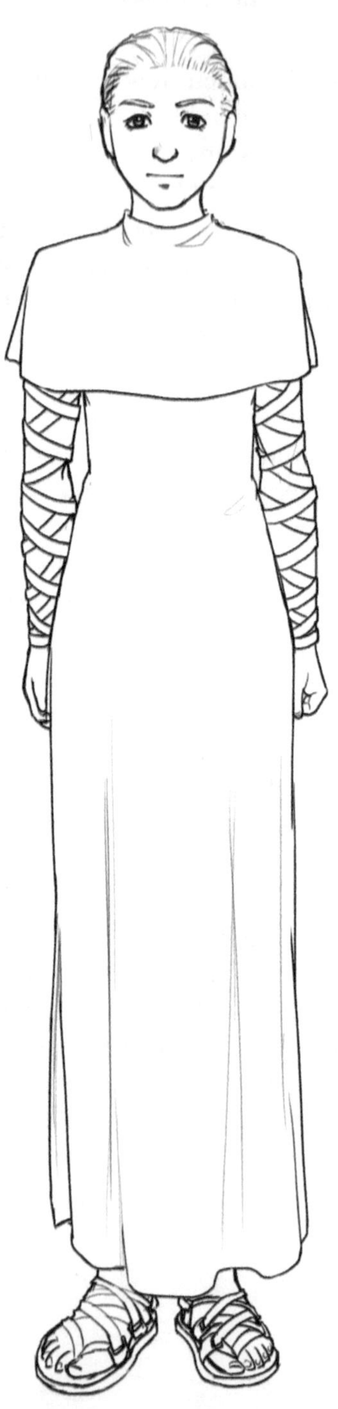

Laenyn Haven Emmerven

CHAPTER TEN

Ray felt Laenyn take control of their body with such speed and ease that it took Ray a moment to realize that she no longer had access to their eyes, their ears—the sensory information she'd taken for granted.

Laenyn! Ray snapped, shoving against the walls Laenyn had put between them. The world opened up again as Laenyn approached the main hall, the sensation of rain on her bare arms and air in her lungs and the scent of earth and sweat overwhelming Ray for a moment before she managed to pull back.

I'm sorry, Laenyn said. *I didn't mean to lock you out of everything. This situation isn't fair to you, either.*

Ray said nothing for a long moment as Laenyn walked into the main hall and sat where Ray had sat for breakfast. Wylwon and Haven sat beside her, pulling off their cloaks; Laenyn had none of her own. Looking down at the table, Ray realized that she had a different cup, one with a chip right at the lip, but the plate was the same—still unwashed.

Do they ever wash?

Clean water is hard to come by. There's no reason to wash plates that have only had fruit on them.

Ray sighed. **You're more likely to get sick if things aren't**

washed after they've been touched.

I'm not likely to get sick at all. I'm Green. Stop distracting me, Ray. I need to be on my guard.

Ray watched out of the corner of Laenyn's eye as an old woman in a robe made of black silk paced down the aisle. Laenyn's skin prickled at her approach, and Ray felt disgust and fury burning on the other side of Laenyn's barrier.

Who's that? Ray asked.

The head of the Council, Laenyn replied. The venom in her voice startled Ray. *Araya Devolair Miria Senea Thyn.*

Did she do something to you?

Laenyn pulled away from Ray, shutting down communications between them. The silence was sudden and unfamiliar; Ray could still sense Laenyn's presence, but had no way of knowing where she was, what she thought, or what she felt. It should have been a relief, but Ray felt wary instead.

That's not fair, Ray said, watching as Araya sat at the farthest table. Laenyn's hand twitched unconsciously, as though her first impulse was to form a fist. Their face was completely blank, though, and no one paid them a second glance. **Laenyn, I have no idea what's going on!**

It might be better that way, Laenyn's voice murmured, too close—Ray stiffened. *There are no innocent women in Ilonon. You can't trust anyone, no matter what they say. Maybe if we weren't in training to be a Keshaan, there'd be more to have faith in, but...* Laenyn's words vanished. Thinking of her own, earlier digression, Ray wondered whether Laenyn might be having similar difficulties.

What do Keshaan do, anyway?

The women with the fruit baskets walked past, doling out two or three lumpy, brown vegetables that looked mostly like potatoes, aside from the purple-ish patches that were as shiny as if they'd been waxed. The woman in yellow leaned over and tipped her jar over their cup, smiling as she poured nothing but air before walking away. Laenyn's face never changed. Ray tried to look at the young girl that sat across from them and to their right, who looked about the same age as Meg had been in Phoenix, but Laenyn resisted her every attempt.

I don't think you know what's at risk here. Laenyn's tone was sharp. *Sit still for ten minutes, would you?*

You won't answer any of my questions, Ray explained.

Laenyn brought one of the vegetables to her mouth and took a bite; it was bland as dirt and sucked the moisture from her mouth. Laenyn swallowed somehow, and brought it to her lips again.

Ray sighed. **Please, Laenyn. I'm curious. I don't know where I am. Is the only danger getting a beating?**

You haven't felt the lash of the wooden switch. Laenyn's voice was full of disdain. *It's no laughing matter. And, no, that's not the only danger. Haven or Mother could be the one to take your beating; you might be the one to have to beat them. That's for the paltry offenses, though. There are always worse punishments, Ray. Don't be such a child.*

I'm ten! Ray said, mostly confident that she'd remembered her age correctly. Things were fading faster with Laenyn around; her own mother's face seemed like a yellowed photograph, almost unrecognizable. What color was Meg's hair? What did her father smell like? She could see an outline in a doorway, and could remember that the smell was important, but she couldn't recall the smell itself.

You're already ten. Look at Haven. She keeps quiet, keeps her head low, knows how to sit still. She's six.

Six? Ray repeated. **I thought she was five.**

You're avoiding my point. I'll answer some of your questions after dinner. Until then, I have to be on my guard.

Laenyn removed Ray's control of their body, forcing her to wait while Laenyn ate. The dry, potato-like vegetables stuck in their throat, but Laenyn kept her face impassive and smooth. The little girl across from them glanced at Laenyn periodically, even though Laenyn never returned the look.

Why does she keep looking at us?

I barely know her, Laenyn sighed internally, managing to swallow another bite. *We're the only Secondary Keshaan, though, even if we're only in training. We stand out.*

How can she tell what your job is?

That's why my hair is dyed. Keshaan must represent their Color in every way. Keshaan wear their hair in braids to keep it out of the way during a fight, and the shoulder covering—the maal—is symbolic as well. Anyone can tell what a person's job is, though; we each have a strict dress code, and we each have to keep our hair in a certain way.

Why?

Why am I answering your questions? Laenyn asked herself. *Never mind her. She's only just turned twelve, so she's not even of apprenticing age yet.*

How do you know that she's twelve? You said that you barely—

She's not wearing a bell, but there's a tan line where it once sat on her neck. She must have turned twelve this spring.

What—

No more questions!

Ray sat back again, wanting to know more, but biting her tongue. The girl kept shooting looks at Laenyn, and when the food caught in Laenyn's throat, she looked concerned. Glancing around the table, she quietly slid her glass of water toward Laenyn. Laenyn made no move to take it, managing to swallow despite her dry throat, though she could feel crumbs sticking in the crevices.

Why don't you take the water? Ray asked, longing for even a tiny sip to ease their dry throat.

It may be a trap. Laenyn spoke simply, picking up the last of the vegetables and raising it to her lips. *Sharing is strictly forbid-*

den. *If it weren't, we all might be pressured to "share" with the Primaries. No one would get their fair part of the crop.*

She can tell you're thirsty. I don't think that—

The girl's cup caught on the gap between the table boards, making a sharp sound. She'd been pushing it slowly enough that it wasn't enough to tip the cup and spill the water, but the woman directly across from Laenyn looked at the girl with stern eyes. The girl hastily withdrew the cup, sloshing it down her front. She leapt a little at the cold—just a little. Just enough to catch the eye of the women at the next table.

"Keep your daughter under control," one of them snapped. Ray recognized the language as Yra as she understood it. "She's nearly an adult! Only infants are that sloppy."

"What is this?" a voice asked, several tables down. Ray recognized the black, wavy hair as she stood: it was the water-bearer. "She's wasting water? This is an insult. I poured that for her myself!"

"What punishment would you ask of me?" the woman across from Ray asked.

That's Sawyn's mother, Keidra. Stop making a fuss, Ray.

She was trying to help you, and now they're talking about punishing her for it! Ray saw the water-bearer smirk for an instant before hiding it.

She broke the rules.

"Ten lashes," the water-bearer replied. Keidra nodded and stood. Sawyn looked ashamed of herself, and turned her back to her mother as she raised her hand. "Ten lashes with the stick," the water-bearer cut in, her eyes like coal. "A mother's hand is too gentle."

"Yes, my lady," Keidra said, her voice tight. Sawyn looked at Laenyn, her eyes pleading, but Laenyn kept her eyes on her plate.

Laenyn, we have to help her! Ray shouted, horror building in her chest as the water-bearer brought over a sharp, wicked-looking rod. **She didn't do anything wrong! This isn't right!**

She broke the rules, Laenyn repeated. Her calm voice made Ray feel nauseous.

Why won't you help her? Ray demanded, her voice getting louder and more desperate as the water-bearer handed the rod to Keidra. **She was just trying to help you!**

She broke the rules. Sawyn has to learn that if you break the rules, you'll be punished. If we speak up, we'll be punished, and it still wouldn't stop anything.

But it isn't right!

Ray wanted to cry, but Laenyn had a rigid hold on their body, paralyzing her. Laenyn didn't flinch as Sawyn lowered the back of her dress to expose her shoulders and back. The rod sang as it whistled through the air, cracking as it met Sawyn's back, leaving a welt that leaked green blood. Sawyn's scream made Ray ram against the walls Laenyn had built around her, unable to bear it.

This isn't right! Ray screamed, trying to make even one of Laenyn's muscles budge. Again, Keidra whipped Sawyn with the flexible, wooden rod—another welt, another cry. Ray felt wild; she'd heard the lash before, but she'd never seen how much it stung, how it bit into the flesh and tore. Sawyn had been trying to help them!

Be quiet, Ray, Laenyn said, her voice icy. *You're behaving like a child again. It's not a big deal.*

Sawyn began to sob as four, sharp lines dripped green blood onto her dress.

"Now one on each shoulder, and two on each leg," the water-bearer said. Sawyn rolled up her sleeves, and Keidra struck. Sawyn stopped screaming, but kept sobbing. Ray saw Meg's face, even though Sawyn looked much younger streaked with tears.

Why is she telling Keidra to...? Ray trailed off, unable to speak.

If the same spot is wounded time and time again, eventually, a person will get used to the pain. Changing the location makes the pain worse.

Ray watched, unable to move or act, as Sawyn pulled up her skirt. Keidra lashed her upper leg, her lower leg; Sawyn's knee tried to buckle beneath her, but she caught herself on the table. Another strike on her other leg, and again—Sawyn sank to the bench, breathing hard, eyes glazed over and red with tears.

"That should teach you not to waste anything," the water-bearer said, taking back the rod. Green blood dripped from it as she turned and strode back to her own table, a satisfied expression on her face.

"I expect that you will clean up your daughter's mess?" a voice asked. It was Araya, the old woman in the black robe.

Her dress absorbed all of the water, Ray said, feeling numb.

But not all of the blood.

CHAPTER ELEVEN

Ray had passed out; Laenyn ignored her. She sat with perfect posture at the table, keeping her eyes on her plate. Haven was shaking beside her. Laenyn couldn't move until she was permitted to go; she couldn't take any of Ray's stupid risks. Stopping a single beating for no real reason? Unfathomable. Laenyn could remember the sting of the lash all too well; she had no desire to feel it again. Sawyn would learn that there were no exceptions to rule-breaking; every slip-up would earn her another beating until she understood that.

Ten slaps could have been a reasonable demand, but the rod was a mite severe. Karylla had probably been raised in a strict home, and, as a Primary, had probably been sent to the little school. Laenyn doubted that Karylla's mother would have struck her own leg rather than harm her daughter. Wylwon was a gentle mother.

It was hard to keep her mind blank after Ray's ruckus. The silence crowded in on Laenyn, making her think more and more to drive it away. Though the Blues and Greens were separated by four other tables, leaving her mostly safe to think as she pleased, she'd had her mind opened to the careless whims of Blues too many times to feel safe.

"You are dismissed for the evening," Lady Araya said. Looking at her made Laenyn dangerously emotional, so she always kept her eyes down when the Lady spoke. Not low enough to accidentally give the impression that she was watching the ground, of course. Watching someone's footprints was a bitter insult: it meant that you were questioning their Color. Laenyn had made that mistake, once, as a child. That was not a mistake that she had ever repeated.

Laenyn waited for Wylwon to stand, then followed her home. The Cotton families left through the east door, which was wide enough to fit five women standing shoulder to shoulder, but it was rare that more than three would pass through at a time. Wylwon, Laenyn, and Haven passed through in a line, giving Sawyn and Keidra a wide berth. Sawyn was limping. Laenyn worried, for a moment, that her wounds would take septic, but brushed it away. Whether they did or not, Sawyn was Green, and more likely to survive an infection than anyone of another Color. Regardless, it was no concern of Laenyn's that she remain in good health.

Are you awake? Laenyn asked Ray. But Ray merely stirred in her sleep, tossing as fitfully as though she was having a nightmare. *Then am I the one who's actually concerned about the girl?* Laenyn could feel the thought, soft though it was, hang inside of her.

Once home, Laenyn climbed the ladder to her loft; Wylwon watched her with concerned eyes, but said nothing as she turned to climb up to her own loft.

"You did much better tonight, Ray," Haven said, her voice shaking as she sat on Laenyn's straw bed. "I don't know how you managed to sit so still."

Laenyn was surprised that she could understand the English, and wasn't confident enough in it to trying speaking it herself.

"I'm your mother, Laenyn," Laenyn said. Haven froze. "Ray would have gotten us into terrible trouble if she'd been free tonight."

"But, how—?" Haven began; she seemed unable to continue.

"I came back when Ray saw Mother strike you," Laenyn explained, sitting beside her.

"So, is Ray...?" Haven gulped. Laenyn felt Ray stir at the sight of Haven's concern, though she remained in her fitful, half-waking sleep.

"We're sharing the body," Laenyn said. Haven's face seemed to fall, though some of the tension in her eyebrows eased. "I am sorry that I left you, even if it was for a short time." Haven leaned against Laenyn's arm, a slight smile on her face.

"I can't be mad at you, Mommy," she said. She kept her voice low enough that passersby would hear nothing. Haven had adapted quickly to Ilonon, especially for a six-year-old. "I'm just so glad that you came back for me. Wylwon really didn't want to hurt me. I slipped in the mud when we were exercising, and Lady Devolair got mad at me. Wylwon's knee is really banged up from trying to protect me. You aren't mad at her, right?"

"Of course not," Laenyn said, stroking Haven's hair. She was warm, especially in contrast with the chilly air. Laenyn wished that they had a blanket to use, as Wylwon had once had, when times were a little kinder to Secondaries. "I saw it in Ray's memories. I know what she was doing. Mother is quite kind at times, isn't she?"

"Yes," Haven said, touching the bright bruise on her face. Her voice was distant. "What else did you see in Ray's memories?"

"Not much," Laenyn said, wrapping her arm around Haven's shoulders and wishing she could offer more. "She calls herself your sister, you know."

"I had a sister named Ray, once," Haven said. She curled inward, wrapping her arms around her legs and pressing herself against Laenyn's side, where Laenyn could feel her trembling. "Please don't make me talk about her, Mommy. This Ray—this can't be the same Ray. If it's the same Ray, then nothing makes sense."

Laenyn nodded. "If you're ready, I think it's time for bed."

"Should we pile up with Wylwon?" Haven asked, pressing a hand against the cloth packed with straw. It was stiff and resisted her touch. "It's already cold, and it's only going to get colder."

"Mother..." Laenyn began, but her voice died in her throat as she remembered Wylwon's concerned eyes. Her expression that made it seem as though she'd given up on Laenyn. Laenyn looked down at her arms and the ribbons that symbolized her obligations to her family. "Has she been worried about me?"

Laenyn glanced up, and Haven bit her lip.

"Yes," she admitted, not able to meet Laenyn's gaze. Her voice was tired and weak. "I heard her crying last night, when she thought I was asleep. I'm pretty sure she blamed herself for what happened to you."

Laenyn sighed, covering her face with her hands. Exhaustion was starting to draw her downward, making her want to curl up and sleep it all off. Ray was sleeping, and Laenyn wanted to follow suit.

"I think it might be best to explain things to Mother in the morning," Laenyn started, but Haven sighed.

"I can run over and explain for you, Mommy," Haven said, yawning. "It's cold, and I want to actually sleep through the night tonight. Wylwon will be glad to have us pile up in this weather, especially once she knows that you're better."

"Mostly better," Laenyn murmured, a pair of proud, unyielding eyes haunting her in the dark. Grief clawed at her chest, too familiar to make her flinch. "Yes, go tell her. Tap the floorboard once when it's time to head over."

Haven grinned and scurried down the ladder, quiet as a mouse. Laenyn turned away and looked down at the floorboards that had been beneath her knees, where a pool of green stained the floor. She knelt and carefully dragged her finger across the wood, leaving words in its wake. It was slow, painstaking work to write; Laenyn only barely knew her letters, and spelling seldom made sense in Yra.

She looked down at what she'd written, almost unwilling to read it. The secret burned in her chest, killing her from the inside, making life a living hell, as it had for so many months. Since before Haven had wandered into Ilonon. Laenyn traced the words again as they began to fade, and then once more after that. The guilt and grief felt like an endless pool of water, drowning her, making her eyes burn and her breaths catch and her movements slow. The thought of standing and walking as far as Wylwon's loft seemed unbearable. All that she wanted in the entire world was to sleep, to sleep on and on until she felt no more.

The words were vanishing. Laenyn began to trace them again, but her hands shook, and her handwriting was nearly illegible. Ray stirred, and Laenyn blotted it all out with a swipe of her hand, burying her secret deep within herself.

Are you all right, Laenyn? Ray asked, sounding half-asleep. **I'm getting a lot of misery over here.**

Laenyn wondered for a moment whether she was the cause of Ray's bad dreams.

You're just dreaming, Ray, she whispered back. Speaking quietly might disguise some of the pain in her voice. *You fell asleep at dinner. We'll all be asleep soon.*

Dinner? Ray repeated groggily. **That girl!** Ray said, waking up suddenly. **Was Sawyn okay? What happened?**

Sawyn was fine, Laenyn replied evenly. *Karylla, the water-bearer, didn't take away any of her rations. She'll be back at meals tomorrow if her mother lets her out of the house. Wait until morning, and you'll see her for yourself.*

Oh, Ray said, and a wave of exhaustion seemed to tug them both gently out into the water. Ray, who had nothing to haunt her, murmured, **Okay...** and was asleep again in an instant. Laenyn felt eyes on her, and the words hidden beneath the smears of green that she'd made seemed burned into her hands.

Haven rapped at the floorboard, and Laenyn stood automatically. There was nothing left for her but obedience. Without that, everything she'd sacrificed to get this far would be lost. She was a Keshaan in training, the oldest of apprentices, the only Secondary Keshaan in Ilonon. Laenyn climbed down the ladder, ignoring her body's creaking weariness.

I'm so close, Laenyn whispered to herself. *I don't even know if I want it any more.*

Laenyn Haven Emmerven

CHAPTER TWELVE

Ray woke to Laenyn meditating in front of the stump.

You slept through breakfast. Sawyn wasn't there; it's usually better to keep a punished child out of sight for a day or two.

What are you supposed to be doing? Ray asked, looking at the stump through Laenyn's eyes. The heavy weight of a wooden staff was more distracting once she'd come into her senses; Laenyn had it balanced across her lap.

Meditating, Laenyn replied.

How is this a job? Ray asked, even though she could feel Laenyn's frustration as she spoke. **Why are you meditating?**

So that I can do this! Laenyn said sharply. An arc of vivid, dark green energy burst from Laenyn's staff to strike the stump, which began to char. With a tug on the staff, she quenched the fire.

But— Ray began, astounded. She gaped at the newly burnt edges of the bark. **But—how? I don't understand!**

Meditation draws your own energy out, allowing you to manipulate it and use it to more purposeful ends. It ages you to draw out your own energy, though, if you don't sleep it off immediately after the fact.

So why use your own energy? Ray asked. An image of

Laenyn aging herself into a withered, old woman made Ray shudder. **If you really need to use energy in the first place, isn't there anything else you can use?**

The wind, Laenyn admitted. There was not even a hint of a breeze. *With more than forty Keshaan and Keshaan-in-training, though, there has been very, very little breeze of late.*

Forty? Ray repeated. **How many women are there in Ilonon, anyway? That seems like a lot of people to have meditating day in and day out.**

Almost one in ten women are Keshaan. Now quit bothering me. This is difficult enough without you.

Women? Ray repeated. **Wait, what about the men? What do the men do?**

Don't be stupid, Laenyn snapped. *Don't you realize that I have to be on my guard while I'm at work?*

I don't even know what your work *is*, Ray replied. **I mean, this energy-magic seems cool, but how useful is it?**

Laenyn gritted her teeth, and her staff burst into dark, sparkling flames that crackled and leapt like lightning around her hands.

There are eight Blue women in the vicinity. Laenyn's tone barely rose above a growl. Fierce annoyance burned across the divide, sending Ray scrambling backward. *Any of them could eavesdrop on these thoughts and call me into questioning. This is not the time to be bothering me with inane questions, Ray!*

Ray said nothing, but watched as Laenyn carefully drew the energy back into her arm.

You sound tired, Ray whispered, as she felt Laenyn settle down and close her eyes. **Did you sleep all right?**

I— Laenyn began in a defensive, snapping tone, then broke off. With a sigh, she continued in a weary voice, *I slept as I usually do, but I typically find myself exhausted well before the end of the day.*

Want me to take over for a while? Ray asked. **You can**

show me what to do, and I can figure things out from there. I know that it's dangerous, but isn't it even more dangerous if you're so tired that you're snapping all the time?

Laenyn hesitated for a long moment before some of the tension eased.

Yes. Laenyn sounded embarrassed. *Yes, of course, you're right. I never had a choice before now. I'm just used to pushing through it all. Somehow, I think I forgot what it was like to... Of course. If you can handle the work, then I'll let you take over.*

Laenyn's relief had a powerful effect on Ray. For a moment, it swept through her, too, easing all of her tension. Then she realized that she'd promised to keep up Laenyn's act without knowing how to do it. She took control anyway, meditating as she'd seen Laenyn meditate.

What else do we do? Ray asked, nerves fluttering in her stomach. Laenyn's tone was that of a sleeping woman, slurred and weary.

If there's an emergency, we'll have to fight. Laenyn yawned. *But there hasn't been a monster attack in the last year. That's why I'm still just a Keshaan apprentice, rather than a full-fledged Keshaan. I have yet to prove myself.*

Laenyn's walls were coming down, leaving her unguarded. Ray hastily erected some of her own, fighting the urge to look around them for women in blue.

What kind of monsters? Ray asked.

The worst is the Haubonalyr, Laenyn said. *The others can usually be dispatched with only a few women, but a Haubonalyr—it can level entire villages.*

How?

It's massive, Laenyn said. Her voice grew drowsier as she continued. *It slithers like a snake, but it rears up to three times as tall as any woman. It's poisonous—though it mostly swallows women whole.* Laenyn's voice trailed away before she caught herself. *But I have to prove myself in battle to graduate from my apprenticeship.*

From Laenyn's side of their mind, Ray felt echoes of loathsome work, shame, exhaustion—it was disorientating enough that she lost her voice for a moment.

I've nearly earned it, Laenyn murmured, half-asleep. *I'm so close...*

Should I wake you if there's... Ray trailed off as she realized that Laenyn was fast asleep. Withdrawing to avoid waking her, Ray opened her eyes, staring at the staff. **Now what do I do with this?** Ray muttered, at a loss. **Laenyn made it work by getting mad, but that'll make us get old. I don't know how to control it.**

Ray stared thoughtfully at the grass, thinking out what little she knew about energy-magic. If she meditated, then it would draw out her own energy, which would make her age. Would taking energy from something else make her get younger? Was it even possible to draw energy out of something other than herself?

Ray closed her eyes, feeling for a breeze. Laenyn had said that was a second option, but there wasn't even the slightest hint of any wind at all.

So much for that, Ray sighed. An idea hit her, and she had to remind herself not to furrow her eyebrows. **Wait. If Laenyn used up our energy by getting mad at me and focusing on herself, maybe I could...** Ray bit her lip, then quickly stopped herself, glancing around. **What if it gets me into trouble?**

But curiosity itched, just under her skin, infuriating and unrelenting. No matter how Ray tried to hold herself still, her fingers twitched against the staff, her feet tapped against the grass, and her mind wouldn't let go of the idea. The sky overhead began to take on a strange blue—the color between dark green and deep purple. Ray felt the idea burning in her chest, and had to swallow to ease the knot in her throat.

Laenyn? Ray asked, her voice timid. **Is it okay if I try something?**

Mmm? Laenyn mumbled, rousing. *What's the matter?*

I kind of had an idea, Ray said, guilt warring with excitement. **Can I try it, or am I going to get into big trouble?**

What's the idea? Laenyn asked, snapping awake. Ray noticed a touch of curiosity behind Laenyn's concern, and shifted uncomfortably.

I want to try taking energy out of the grass, Ray said. **I want to put it into that little gray flower there.**

Out of the grass? Laenyn repeated, astonished. *That's not a technique that I've ever seen in use. It's like sacrilege, isn't it? The earth is full of impurity. Only the air and skies are clean—it's so hard to even think to draw it from the earth. What made you consider it?*

I don't want to make us age, Ray said. **Will I get in trouble? Can I try it?**

Laenyn balked for a moment, then pulled back to think. Ray waited impatiently, knowing that soon the sky would be dark and she would lose her chance. Finally, Laenyn returned. Even before she spoke, Ray knew her answer.

I'll help you, Laenyn said. Ray grinned, barely suppressing their body's lips.

Ray focused on the grass. **I just have to get mad at it, right?** Ray asked. What about it could make her angry? Suddenly, a cloud shifted out of the way of the light, and daylight hit the ground. The grass was a vivid, fiery red—it curled up the stump, thin as hair and just as soft. Inexplicable, inescapable anger rose in Ray's chest, scaring her enough that she almost dropped their staff. It looked like Haven's hair, and Ray felt an old hatred roiling in her heart. It wasn't Laenyn—it wasn't even her, not really. It was something that should have felt familiar—it was like seeing her face scowling at her out of the mirror when she was grinning. Terror drew needles down Ray's spine.

Calm down, Laenyn said. *I can't believe it's working! You don't have to panic. How are you doing this? You haven't even been trained!*

Ray looked again, fighting down the bile in her throat, and joy washed all the terror and rage out of her. The grass shriveled on the stump's right side, wilting and browning away into nothing as tiny threads of energy arced between the blades of grass. Ray held out her free hand, palm downward, fingers extended. Slowly, with Laenyn's urging, she curled them inward, making a fist. Nothing happened.

Think about gathering them as you try again, Laenyn said, her thoughts hushed with eagerness. Ray nodded and tried again, managing it with Laenyn's joint control of their hand.

Now, the flower, Laenyn said. *Gently, gently. Those little threads are weak.*

Ray painstakingly moved her hand to the left. The little, gray flower was on the other side of the stump. A single thread of energy broke off from the bundle, falling to land on the stump like a spark. It lit up as it hit the stump, bursting into a dozen glittering shards. Swallowing, Ray eased the rest of the energy into the flower. It drew its petals inward, budding and turning a brighter shade of green as it shrank downward, swallowing its own leaves.

Wow, Ray breathed, releasing the rest of the energy. The flower was just a green tendril in a sea of red grass. **It... It really worked. Can I put the energy back in the grass?**

Laenyn took control and fumbled for the energy inside the flower. She drew out an amount that looked about as big as what she'd put in, but the flower sprouted too quickly—it looked sickly and wilted, hanging limply on a sagging stem. Though Laenyn pressed the energy back into the grass, most of it just flickered out. Only a few blades of grass perked up, turning a reddish color the hue of dried blood as Ray remembered it—the rest smoldered, tiny sparks eating away at the edges as thin tendrils of smoke wound toward the sky.

That poor flower, Ray murmured, sorry that she'd killed it and the grass. **Why couldn't we put it back, Laenyn?**

I think it's a matter of practice, Laenyn said. There was nothing but a cool, intellectual interest in her voice. *Maybe I drew the energy out in the wrong way. Maybe the flower needs to use it in the right way to make itself grow. Maybe we took too much from the grass in the first place. I can't believe that it worked, Ray. What made you think of such a bizarre idea?*

It doesn't seem bizarre to me, Ray said, glancing up at the deepening sky before looking back at the little patch of dead grass and the sickly flower. **It was the next logical step.**

Laenyn shook her head in their mind space.

Not in Ilonon, she murmured. *We were taught to look at the energy-magic as the purity in life. Life is usually the antithesis of purity and peace. Wind is a pure life-force: it doesn't rely on the earth for sustenance. We are impure and imperfect, but our minds are fed by the moons rather than the earth, so we can draw the energy from there. Thinking of the grass as having that same energy— that was so shocking! That it should have life, just as a human does. I can't believe it!*

That doesn't—

IT IS TIME TO GO, the Blue woman said, her voice sharp. I WILL WATCH YOU AND YOUR FAMILIES AT DINNER. KESHAAN SHOULD BE THE BEST OF THEIR COLOR; DO NOT EVER DISAPPOINT ME, NOR EVER LET YOUR FAMILY DISAPPOINT ME. INITIATION CEREMONIES ARE CLOSE AT HAND.

Ray let Laenyn take control and watched as Laenyn's eyes lingered on the grass and flower. Pride and delight glowed in Laenyn's chest, unmistakable. Too many walls were down to hide it; Ray's were more permeable than Laenyn's. Gradually, though, as the words sank in, it turned into bitterness. As the glow congealed into a cold resentment, Laenyn's grip grew tighter on her staff. Her knuckles were white when she turned away, maintaining perfect posture.

There's no point, anyway, Laenyn said sharply. The happy daze that she'd woken to had clearly faded. Regret bit at Ray's heart. *They'll never change their ways. If they see me trying new things, then...* Laenyn's throat tightened; Ray felt the tears pricking at her eyes, but they didn't swell. The grip Laenyn maintained on their expression was absolute. *There's no point.*

It can be our secret, Ray offered, trying to give Laenyn back some of the hope that had died at the sound of the Blue woman's thoughts. **Just because no one else is willing to try it doesn't mean that we can't experiment with it.**

Secrets! Laenyn scoffed. *Jauge is the one who experiments. I was foolish.*

Ray felt the world swaying around her, and suddenly realized that Laenyn's walls had gone up, shutting her out so sharply that Ray felt dizzy. She hadn't realized how much she'd been relying on Laenyn's energy to get by.

I'm sorry, Ray whispered, thinking of the terrible rage she'd felt. Everything was distorted; her hands felt wet and sticky, and there was a scent in the air that she might have named—it was just on the tip of her tongue when Laenyn turned her attention toward Ray, disrupting the illusion like so much smoke before the wind.

Are you all right? Laenyn asked. *I didn't mean to offend...*

Ray sank, though the walls parted a crack and she could feel Laenyn's realization on the other side.

The energy-magic, Laenyn said. *Oh, Ray, I just left it all on you,* Laenyn's voice sounded like bubbles searching for the surface, distant and barely understandable. *You had no way to even know that it would wear...*

Ray slipped away, and Laenyn's voice went out in a wink.

Model by Jeff Miller

Wylwon Laenyn Emmerven

CHAPTER THIRTEEN

Laenyn paced back and forth, careful to mind how loudly her feet fell against the floor. Haven's eyes were on her, but Wylwon had not yet returned home. Laenyn's head ached.

"Are you all right, Mommy?" Haven asked tentatively. "You look upset."

I'm not sure. Laenyn sighed, stopping and covering her face with her hands. *I'm not used to feeling—like this. Ray's so full of vigor and emotion. I don't know how to deal with this. It was so easy to just follow my orders, to keep myself from questioning any-thing. I haven't felt like crying in years. I haven't wanted to smile in years. This is too much to handle.*

Aloud, she said, "Of course. Don't worry about me." She un-covered her face and looked up at Haven, trying to ease the lines in her brow. There was no use in making Haven fret. "How was your day?"

"I sat around," Haven said. "Practiced stretching so I won't slip again." Haven felt the bruise on her cheek gingerly. "There's not much to do during the day, since I'm not in school."

"I don't want you to go to school," Laenyn said, knowing that no Green had been admitted to the school in the last two decades, let alone a Cotton Green. "It's not safe."

"I know," Haven said, sitting back against the wall. "Especially since I wasn't born here, right? That's why I have to be really careful."

Laenyn nodded, heart heavy. Ray stirred in her sleep, and Laenyn's heart leapt.

Ray? Are you awake?

Ray slipped away again, and Laenyn sat down. Her head seemed stuffed with cotton—using energy-magic had taken its toll on her, too. Even so, it was always worse for beginners, and Ray had gone in without knowing what a drain it would enact on her own energy. Laenyn hadn't thought to warn her. She'd known from her first day of training that the work would be exhausting.

Ray had asked her what a Keshaan's job was. Repressing a shudder, Laenyn tried to think of an answer that would capture it all. Certainly Ray would ask again, and keep asking. What about the men? Why do the Colors mean anything? What stupid questions! It was as pointless as asking why the sky got dark at night. Because the moons had decreed it! Because it was all Laenyn had ever known!

Somehow, I doubt that you would be satisfied with such answers, Laenyn sighed, envying Ray's sleep. The front door slid open, and Wylwon walked in. As she shut the door behind her, her downcast face became a brilliant grin.

"Laenyn!" she said, rushing forward to take Laenyn's hands, looking eagerly up into her eyes. "I have discovered the most marvelous thing!" Wylwon bit her lip and flushed with embarrassment before continuing in a hushed tone, leading Laenyn toward the closet. "You, too, Haven. Lake Anonwe holds so many secrets! I learn something new every day."

They shut the closet door behind them, and Wylwon pulled out the satchel that she always carried, hidden, in the folds of her dress. Her dress was similar to that of the Council members in that it was simple and tied together with a strip of cloth. However, the Council members' dresses were held by a wide, thick band of silk, and had carefully made sleeves. Wylwon's was a thick, cotton cloth that had to be artfully draped across her shoulders.

Laenyn shook herself awake. Such digressions could be dangerous, as they made her lose track of time and the world around her. Wylwon dug through her satchel, pulling out a spiral-shaped shell.

"Do you see this?" Wylwon asked, holding it out to them. It was a nondescript white, very similar in color to the dusty dirt that was prevalent in Ilonon. Laenyn and Haven nodded, glancing briefly at one another, and Wylwon grinned. "No, you don't. Not truly." Wylwon's voice was bursting with pride; she set the shell down carefully, pulling away her hands for dramatic effect. Wylwon's green streaks appeared on the shell as surely as they might on wood or soil. Haven gasped. "It is the same," Wylwon said. "The very same as the soil, I mean. I have done so many tests today; there were more than a dozen abandoned shells in one area. When crushed time and again by a foot, they become utterly indistinguishable from the soil!"

"What does that mean?" Laenyn asked, carefully lifting the shell and looking at it.

"It means that we have an incorrect understanding of the soil!" Wylwon exclaimed. Biting her lip again, she lowered her voice. "It means—oh, Laenyn, it means a great deal. Some have said that dark soil, as is found in other parts of the world, is more nutritious than our own soil, and that the paleness of it is due to overworking it. Some have said that dark soil is tainted by the impurity of other villages. There are so many hypotheses—they don't matter."

"Why not?" Laenyn asked, knowing that it would please Wylwon. Wylwon's grin made her heart lighter.

"Because this implies that our soil is not made of decomposing plant matter, but crushed shells! It would explain the consistency, the nutritious properties, the..." Laenyn stopped listening, though she kept her face engaged, nodding and making sounds at appropriate times

Though she hid her intelligence well in public, science was Wylwon's passion in life, a passion that was ill-rewarded by the Council. That was the reason that Laenyn had decided to become a Keshaan. Her own prestige could protect her mother from the Council's disapproval. Scientists were only a step above inventors like Jauge on the social ladder.

If only I had any opportunity to become a full-fledged Keshaan. Laenyn thought, wishing that Ray would reply, even if only to ask another inane question. *I've been training myself for so long.* She didn't dare voice the sacrifices she'd made; it was hard enough to think back on the last five years of her life without that.

Ray shifted in her sleep, just barely reaching consciousness. Laenyn kept one ear trained on Wylwon's ramble, but turned the other inward, listening for Ray.

You never did explain anything, Ray muttered. Laenyn wanted to laugh—the desire was startling.

No, Laenyn admitted, *Not really. How are you feeling?*

Like shit. Ray laughed. **I'm sorry that I got you so worked up over that flower, Laenyn. But can't we call it a success anyway? It doesn't have to matter to anyone other than us, does it?**

Laenyn smiled a little, looking at Wylwon's enormous grin, watching as she gesticulated when she couldn't find the words to explain herself. Wylwon's discovery would never reach the ears of the Council. They couldn't care less about the source of the soil; it was only the use of the existing soil that mattered to them.

I suppose that you're right. Laenyn's voice was low. *The Keshaan teachers would beat me if they knew that I'd tried something new without permission, you know. Not the tame sort of beating that you saw last night, either.*

Ray gulped, but managed to imply a shrug. **At least no one saw us.**

Wylwon launched into an explanation—mostly for Haven's

sake—about the theories behind why Color drew pigment out of so many sources. The mystic views that Wylwon's mother had drilled into Laenyn were of no interest to Wylwon. Her experiments had been inconclusive, but she suspected that it had to do with sweat; the effect lasted longer on hot days. But clean water made no difference in prolonging the impression, so it couldn't have anything to do with the moisture content... As Wylwon started to go into depth about secretions, Laenyn retreated.

When will you answer my questions?

Laenyn glanced at the window paper, which had darkened to a bluish-purple.

After dinner.

CHAPTER FOURTEEN

Ray was getting familiar enough with the rituals around dinner that Laenyn gave her control long enough to take a little nap of her own. Sawyn sat across from her tonight, not looking anywhere near her. Ray's heart went out to her, but she didn't dare look at her or make any expression of comfort. There was no murmuring in the room, no shifting, no clinking of plates and cups, not even the quiet ringing of the girls' bells. A dark tension permeated the crowd, building as the women quietly set out fruit. No water-bearers appeared.

The old woman in black silk, Araya, stood. Her face seemed suddenly inhuman, though it was hard to explain why. It was something in the glint of her eyes, the curve of her teeth.

"I have heard reports of disrespect," Araya said, her voice clear and penetrating. There was nothing elderly about it. "Disrespect toward the water-bearers, certainly, but other reports have reached my ears as well. Reports of discontent." The word rang like a death knell. As one, the entire room shrank backward. Laenyn woke in an instant, taking control.

Somebody wants to start a rebellion? Ray asked. **Well, this place is—**

Laenyn snipped off her thought without hesitation. Blue

women lined the walls, one to each end of a table. Practicing her meditation, Laenyn kept her mind blank, and she fought to keep her heart steady. A fearful heart was a sign of guilt.

"This Council is given power by its people," Araya said. "Should any wish to object, your voices will be heard and considered." Laenyn's mouth felt dry; she knew that she would never dare to speak up here. "Without any such appeals, however, I believe that it is time to examine all of you. Those who have done no wrong should have no fear."

Laenyn made herself breathe evenly. No one nearby seemed to be breathing; Laenyn realized that she could not hear anything, including her own breaths.

LAENYN HAVEN EMMERVEN, the Blue woman addressed her. She was the head Keshaan instructor, Dayan Kevair Illen; Laenyn recognized her voice immediately. DO I HAVE PERMISSION TO LOOK THROUGH YOUR MIND?

Of course, my lady, Laenyn said, allowing her in and hoping desperately that Ray would remain hidden in the pocket of memory into which Laenyn had corralled her. Lady Dayan was meticulous, but not brutal. There were worse women to allow into her mind. Laenyn kept her heart stony, her face blank. Ray's emotions were difficult to fight, but she had trained herself to drop all emotion when she became a Keshaan-in-training, and she felt nothing as she watched Lady Dayan run her hands all over her heart.

GOOD, Lady Dayan said. YOU BEAR NO GUILT IN THIS MATTER. I WOULD HAVE HAD TO KILL YOU MYSELF, AND IT WOULD HAVE BEEN A TERRIBLE STAIN ON THE ESTEEMED HISTORY OF KESHAAN. LET US HOPE THAT YOUR FAMILY IS EQUALLY BLAMELESS. EVEN IF THEY ARE NOT, YOU ARE CLEARLY NO ACCOMPLICE OF THEIRS.

Thank you, my lady, Laenyn said, waiting until she had fully withdrawn to breathe a sigh of relief, and waiting until Lady Dayan had moved well past her in the line to release Ray.

What's going on? Ray asked, and Laenyn was relieved to

hear her whisper rather than shout.

This isn't uncommon, Laenyn explained. *If there is the slightest suspicion of rebellion, they examine us. We are in no danger if we are utterly blameless.*

She saw me, Ray said, shuddering. Laenyn froze. **That blue-haired woman. She looked me right in the eye, and I really thought I was going to die.**

A terrible stain... Laenyn murmured, remembering what Lady Dayan had said. She swallowed. *I don't think that Lady Dayan would admit to finding something she doesn't understand, especially in the heart of one of her hand-picked Keshaan apprentices.*

Lady Araya listened to the Blue women, nodding. No one in the room was writhing in pain, so it seemed that there was no substance to the reports that Araya had heard. Ray kept close to Laenyn, drawing comfort from her stoicism.

"It seems that all of you are content after all," Araya said, smiling toothfully at the crowd, but looking wholly unsatisfied. "Water-bearers!"

Every cup was filled to the point of overflowing. Ray noticed that Karylla wasn't smiling tonight; every face had the pall of fear on it. Laenyn kept her hands steady, and didn't spill as she brought the cup to her lips. Haven didn't even reach for hers; her fingers were nearly trembling too hard to lift up the fruit on the plate before her. The fruit was green and fuzzy, shaped like a lemon, but at least three times the size.

An aewymn. Laenyn explained. *Last night we ate kot-ol.*

The aewymn was soft and sour. Ray gagged on the half-inch long fuzz, but Laenyn ate it without hesitation. The juice was thick like pus and stuck to the roof of Laenyn's mouth.

It's good for us. Stop complaining.

Ray withdrew from their mouth, not wanting to taste it any more, but it was too difficult to pull away from just the touch senses that were affected in Laenyn's mouth; she had to give up the sensation of wood beneath them, the texture of their dress, the cold that seeped through the soles of their very worn shoes. It was like a dream without the myriad, tiny textures cluing her in on the world around her.

Araya paced down the aisles between the tables, her gaze like that of a wolf. Ray was relieved, for once, that Laenyn avoided meeting everyone's eyes. Araya sent chills down her spine, even as red hot anger split Laenyn's own chest. Noting Dayan at Araya's side, Ray didn't dare ask Laenyn any questions.

"You are dismissed," Araya said, well before anyone had actually finished their food. Her voice had a bite in it; her eyes darted from face to face, half-wild. "Leave what you have not finished. It will be used as fertilizer for the next crop."

Haven had only just stilled her hands long enough to lift her fruit, and she set it down with regret in her eyes. Wylwon had finished almost as much as Laenyn had. Out of the corner of Laenyn's gaze, Ray caught her slipping the fruit into her dress behind Araya's back. Laenyn clenched a fist momentarily, but said nothing.

What's she doing? Ray asked. **Araya said to leave the food.**

Laenyn flashed the image of Dayan at Araya's side in response, and Ray quieted herself. She couldn't meditate the way that Laenyn could, but she tried. Ray hadn't walked home in the darkness that fell during dinner before; she'd been unconscious the previous night. The air was cold and crisp, without even the slightest hint of a breeze, and the sky above them was a deep purple, dotted with bright stars. The moons were beautiful, especially the black moon—it was barely visible in the dark purple, but it was somehow incredible.

The Gray Moon protects Secondaries, Laenyn whispered to her, turning their gaze away from the sky. *The Black Moon may take insult if you stare too long. Mind yourself.*

And the White Moon? Ray asked. **Who does it help?**

Only itself, Laenyn replied, sighing. *Itself and its own. Only the Whites pray to it. No one else would dare.*

They walked briskly, though they were outpaced by several women that went past the Green row. It was too dark to detect the color of their dresses.

I haven't seen any men, Ray whispered, the realization hitting her as she watched the women pass them. **Where are they?**

Below ground, of course, Laenyn replied. Her tone was so matter-of-fact that her words didn't register for a moment. When they did, Ray froze.

What, like, dead? Ray squeaked.

Something akin to it, in its own way, Laenyn said. There was a note of envy in her voice that made Ray uneasy. *They're sent to the Underground Caverns as soon as they're born.*

Why? Ray demanded. A weight settled in Laenyn's chest— Ray felt it for an instant before Laenyn drew back.

They're not allowed to see the skies, Laenyn said. *They were the agents of the first rebellion; it's punishment for their treachery.*

And you think that's fair?

The Caverns aren't so bad, Laenyn said. Her voice was almost wistful. *There's no Council listening. It could be much worse.*

Ray imagined being trapped underground, confined for as far back as she could remember. Laenyn's body suddenly felt too restrictive; she wanted to take control and leave Ilonon far behind her.

There's no escape, Laenyn said. *Deserters are a personal insult to the Council; they chase them down and tear them to pieces.*

Then do something about it! Realization hit Ray, and she shuddered, pulling away from Laenyn. **You can't just—just wait to die!**

Laenyn said nothing for a long, quiet moment.

I'll explain once we're inside, she said. *Treasonous thoughts could be the death of us all.*

CHAPTER FIFTEEN

They shut the door firmly behind them, and Wylwon motioned for them to follow her into the closet. Once inside, Wylwon fished the second half of her aewymn from inside her robe, holding it out to Haven, whose eyes went wide.

"Oh, Wylwon," she murmured. "You're going to get in trouble."

"You didn't get any dinner," Wylwon replied, kneeling to look Haven in the face. "What did they say to you that terrified you so?"

Haven looked away sharply. "I—I'm forbidden from saying," she whispered. Wylwon pressed the fruit into her hands, and Haven looked back at her. Offering her a grin, Wylwon wrapped her hands around Haven's, making them close around the fruit.

"No matter what it may be, Laenyn can protect you from it," she whispered. Haven's eyes seemed startlingly bright, almost as though she was starting to cry. "You can tell me if you need to talk to someone. Laenyn is around Blues far more often than I am." Wylwon clapped her on the shoulder, grinning. "In any case, that's your dinner. Children need food to grow. You're much smaller than Laenyn was at your age. Eat up, and then get a good night's sleep."

With that, Wylwon waved her hand and left, offering Laenyn a parting smile instead of a good night. Haven leaned back against the wall heavily, staring down at the squished fruit.

"That was reckless of her," Laenyn groaned, leaning against the wall opposite Haven. "Make sure to finish it. Wylwon may get a beating for sneaking that food to you."

"I know," Haven whispered, still turning the fruit over in her hands. She took a tentative bite, and Ray winced at the memory of the pus-like juice, but Haven smiled. "That was awfully kind of her."

"Go on up and sleep beside her," Laenyn said, sensing Ray's frustration. "I'll be up after explaining some things to Ray."

"Good night, Mommy," Haven smiled. "G'night, Ray."

"Good night," Laenyn said, almost smiling in return. She watched Haven as she slipped back out the door, then dropped the smile and turned inward.

You have questions, Laenyn said. Ray crossed her arms as Laenyn closed their eyes; only the mindscape remained. *Ask them.*

Ray almost continued their previous conversation, but one question had filled her since she'd emerged from that lake.

How did I get here? Ray asked. Laenyn turned away from her. **Why am I here?**

I don't know where you came from, Laenyn said carefully. *And I don't know how Jauge built the device that found you; I'm not a scientist. If you want to find your way home, you'll have to ask someone else.*

Ray thought back to the lake—and a crippling headache crushed her, halting all thought. It blistered like a burn beneath her skin, knotting in the folds of her brain—unbearable.

Ray? Laenyn asked. The pain went away, and Ray stared up at Laenyn. Ray didn't want to trigger the pain again.

So men are the bottom of the chain? Ray asked. She though of her own father—a silhouette in a doorway and a scent she couldn't quite recall any more. **No one ever meets their fathers?**

If they do, they don't speak of it, Laenyn said. *Only hybrids are lower than men.*

Hybrids?

They are very few in number, Laenyn said. *Tests are done on newborns to check their blood. We're only meant to have one Color—babies with more are put to death.*

Ray recoiled.

Put to *death*? she repeated. There had to be an explanation—some sort of reason. **Does—does it hurt, having more than one Color? Would they die anyway?**

No.

Ray thought of the kids she'd seen being hurt so far—thought of Wylwon beating her own leg in a bizarre attempt to protect Haven.

Why?

Hybrids aren't human, Laenyn replied, and Ray felt that she'd struck a sore spot. Laenyn's pain and grief washed over her, but Ray didn't want to back down.

And you believe that? Who told you to believe it—your precious Council?

White and blue flecks splashed across Ray's vision; they clung to Laenyn's hands as she pulled away from Ray.

I can believe nothing else!

So you think that they should die?

Laenyn's hair came free of her illusory braid; she looked horrified as she withdrew into a corner to guard her back, then dropped the illusion, vanishing from their mindspace.

If they aren't killed at birth, they grow into women. Women who don't have a family—women who go on to birth more hybrids. There is no place for hybrids in Ilonon!

You do! You think that it's right to kill them!

There's no choice in the matter. They cannot live in Ilonon. If they fled—have you ever met a hybrid, Ray?

No, Ray admitted. **It doesn't matter—**

They aren't like us, Laenyn cut in. *They aren't human. You don't understand!*

Wouldn't Green be a hybrid? Ray sneered. **Yellow and Blue make Green, don't they?**

No. Our Colors don't blend—they haven't since the days of the Legend. Yellow and Blue make Yellow-Blue; a hybrid with endless energy and the ability to read minds. Something not intended by creation.

No one chooses to be born! Ray felt something like a memory brush against her, too vague and indistinct to interpret clearly; water pressed down on her lungs, suffocating her.

I think we should sleep, Laenyn said. *I don't know what I can tell you—I don't know how to make you understand.*

I will *never* understand, Ray hissed. **I don't care if a baby has two Colors or ten.**

Laenyn took control of their body and stood.

It's cold, she said. *We should pile up with Mother and Haven.*

Ray said nothing, curling up to swallow her rage and righteous indignation. She was beginning to realize why Laenyn had gotten so upset earlier in the day. As Laenyn climbed nimbly up the ladder to Wylwon's loft, Ray had to bite back tears.

Yes, Laenyn murmured. She curled up beside Haven, regret rolling through her. *Ilonon is completely without hope.*

CHAPTER SIXTEEN

The morning light woke Ray before Laenyn. Wylwon shifted a moment later, and Ray grimaced, unwilling to wake up and face another day of this. The reality that she might not have a home waiting for her somewhere was starting to dawn on her, and living through months and years of facing Ilonon loomed before her—an insurmountable challenge.

"Good morning, Laenyn," Wylwon murmured, pulling away. The morning air had winter's frosty bite; Ray shivered. Wylwon yawned. "Good morning, Haven."

"Morning," Haven replied, sitting up and stretching.

"Morning," Ray said, careful to use Yra rather than English. She stretched her hands over her head, noting the taut muscles. Laenyn was powerful—each muscle had been carefully trained, and Ray could feel the memory of energy-magic. Could she use that power to tear down the stupid laws that made everyone live in constant terror? Could she use it to rebuild Ilonon so that it was a safe place for everyone—not just the Primaries?

The Blue women would paralyze you before you even began a fight, Laenyn said quietly. *There's no point in even considering it. Whatever power we may have, they have more. They can read our every thought if they suspect us, and they won't hesitate to punish us. Don't think dangerous thoughts, Ray.*

How can you stand it? Ray asked, getting up to follow Haven and Wylwon to breakfast. Her dress was still stiff from the lake water, even after two days. Ray felt unclean; she wanted to scrub the dirt and sweat away. She smelled like a locker room.

Stand what? Laenyn asked. *We don't have enough water to bathe more than once a month, Ray.*

That's not what I meant, Ray said, embarrassed that it had been on her mind. **What we talked about last night. How can you stand it?**

I don't understand you, Laenyn replied. *There's nothing to stand for; things are the same as they have been since the time of the Legend.*

Squinting into the bright daylight overhead—the daylight that had no source, no sun—Ray felt utterly removed from the world around her. Nothing fit the way that she wanted it to fit.

I want to go home, she whispered. **Isn't there any way to send me back?**

Laenyn hesitated. Ray told herself that it was because Laenyn knew as little about their situation as Ray herself, but the truth lurked behind Laenyn's tone.

Ask... Ask Jauge. Laenyn replied. *She's the only one who knows anything any more.*

Haven knew me, Ray replied. The thought, 'I'm real!' went unvoiced, as did, 'And Haven hated me.'

Yes, Laenyn said, stopping to take control of their face, which Ray had neglected. Ray pulled back to let her take control of the entire body, not wanting to deal with Ilonon, wanting desperately to go back home, where she had Meg, her mother, and her father—where she'd had Haven. How much time had passed? All of Ray's memories were growing cloudy.

Ray shook herself to dissipate the chill that was twining around her stomach. Laenyn was at the breakfast hall; details leapt out at Ray, like the lines in the worn wood, the weave of the velvet dresses on women nearby, the scent of something coppery and foul and so familiar it made her sick to her stomach, though she couldn't place it. Haven's hair caught the light; she wore a clay bell on a choker around her neck. In the morning light, the clay shone like bronze.

Are you all right, Ray? Laenyn asked. Ray felt as though she was sinking into a warm embrace; there was something comforting about the idea of letting her eyes close, letting herself drift off...

"Stupid Lower!" a woman snapped, towering over a small girl that lay prone and sniffling on the floor. "Watch where you're walking!"

Ray? Laenyn repeated. The world seemed to sharpen as Ray snapped out of her daze and woke up fully. *Did you sleep well last night?*

No, Ray answered. She'd dreamt of Phoenix, and her family, but the dream slipped through her fingers, almost impossible to recall. **I hope that I see Jauge today. I want to ask her how I can get home.**

Don't ever hope to see Jauge, Laenyn said, glancing briefly at the White table to their far right, where two rows of women sat across from one another. Every woman and child had white hair and cat eyes to identify them. Ray doubted that she'd need to see their white dress to recognize them in a crowd. Looking from the door, the rows of tables seemed shorter; there were hardly a dozen women on each side of the White table, aside from some number of children.

There are, what, four hundred women in Ilonon?

Four hundred forty-six women that are of age. Women come of age for the first time at the age of twelve, when their bells are removed. They come of age again at fifteen, when they begin apprentice work. The final coming-of-age step is to bear a child.

What if a woman doesn't want kids? Ray asked. Laenyn shifted slightly at the table as a fruit-bearer held out her breakfast. Laenyn set her hand on the table, and Ray realized that Laenyn was showing the women her Color to get her food and water. Ray shuddered.

All women must bear children, Laenyn replied, her voice barely even. *Between the ages of seventeen and twenty-three, each woman must bear at least one daughter.*

What happens if someone refuses? Ray asked. **Or if they can't?**

Then they're left in the Underground Caverns to live with the men. Laenyn's voice was flat, and she began to eat the aewymn before her. *If a woman can prove that she is infertile, she may return, but has to wear a head covering that masks her face, and she is permanently marked as half a woman.*

Ray felt sick. **I don't want to talk about this any more.**

Good.

Ray withdrew as Laenyn ate, not wanting to see any more beatings that she would be helpless to halt. Out of the corner of Laenyn's eye, Ray watched Haven. Haven had always been quiet in Phoenix, too; Ray remembered that. Ray could remember a lot about Haven, if she tried. If she tried to consider how she'd gotten to Ilonon, or inquired too deeply about how to return, those abominable headaches might come back.

Why had Haven hated Ray so much?

That question nagged at Ray. Haven hadn't spoken to her for any length of time since Laenyn had come back, so Ray hadn't had the opportunity to ask. Ray could remember as much about Haven as she could about herself—the way that Haven had lived in constant fear, had felt entirely as though she couldn't belong. The way that Ray had bullied her, thinking it normal for an older sister to mistreat her younger sister in the name of seniority and —something else, something that she couldn't quite remember. Ray remembered the anger from before, that had come from somewhere else and tried to consume her, and she wondered whether that anger really had consumed her in Phoenix.

What was her older sister's name?

Ray panicked. Though she knew that she had an older sister, that sister's name and face eluded her. What color were her eyes and hair? What shape was her face? How tall was she? Ray had no idea. Her sister might pass her on the street, and she wouldn't recognize her.

Her mother, father! Ray scrambled to recall their faces, the sound of their voices, their scent. It was like looking at worn outlines—anyone might fit their roles. Ray's heart pounded as she closed off the outside world to look inward. Who was her sister? Haven was the only one that she could see, looking away from Ray with tears in her eyes and bruises along her arms. Who was her mother? Wylwon was the only face she could pull up, the only tangible person that she could attach to the concept. Had she ever truly had a father or older sister? There was no one in Ilonon to take their places; Ray wanted to vomit, to get the emptiness outside herself. She wanted to scream until the memories came back.

I am Ray, I am Ray, I am Ray, Ray whispered to herself, her voice the only familiar thing that she had left. If she lost that, she might lose everything—the edges of her mind seemed to be collapsing, shrinking, pulling in on her. **I am Ray!** Ray shouted. **I am Ray, I am Ray, I am Ray!** The walls ground to a halt, and Ray was left gasping for air.

Ray? Laenyn asked. *Are you all right?*

Ray looked around. Where was Haven? But slowly their surroundings sunk in, and she realized that she was kneeling before the old, charred stump. It felt as though she'd just surfaced; her lungs burned for air. Laenyn took over.

Why are you breathing so hard? Laenyn demanded. *What's going on?*

Tell me my name, Ray whispered, her voice hoarse and raw and terrified. **Tell me the name of my older sister. Tell me what my mother and father looked like.**

Laenyn hesitated, and Ray felt her unease through the borders between them before Laenyn brought up more walls to keep them apart.

Your name is Ray, Laenyn said, taking a tone that Ray hadn't yet heard—it was as though Laenyn was trying to soothe an animal. *Your sisters are Meg and Haven. I can't tell you the rest, because I don't know it. What's going on?*

Meg, Ray repeated. The name felt like something she'd heard in a dream. Slowly, her heart eased. **My older sister was named Meg. That's right.**

Ray?

Ray let out a deep, shuddering breath that Laenyn barely masked from Ilonon.

I'm ten, right? Ray asked. **I'm short, with green eyes and brown hair?**

Yes, that's how you've always presented yourself.

Ray breathed deeply through her nose, letting it out through her mouth. The air smelled clean and crisp, like grass and rain. Recognizing the smells set Ray's heart at ease. She didn't dare question what Laenyn was telling her for fear that the world would start breaking down around her again.

Okay. I can live with that.

Laenyn seemed wary as Ray opened her eyes to their mind space, with its endless white floor and formlessness.

We're training right now, Laenyn said. *I know that you want to talk to Haven, but you'll have to wait. I'm—I'm sorry that I wanted you to shut up. I didn't know anything was wrong until you started shouting.*

You were distracted, Ray said. She didn't want to think about it; she wanted a distraction of her own. **Can we practice that trick with the grass again?**

I think it would be a bad idea. If we were caught experimenting, we could face a rather severe punishment.

So we're just pretending to meditate? Ray asked. Laenyn nodded. **At least tell me more about the Colors. I know what Blue and Black do,** Ray remembered Dayan in their mind, Araya with her ever-changing face. **And you told me that Purple can make things float, and that Green lets us stay healthy. There are other Colors, too. And you never explained why they're ranked the way that they are.**

If I tell you every Color, you'll forget them all, or mix them all up. Laenyn seemed a little relieved, though; the tension in her brow faded. *That's common in children who haven't experienced much interaction with women of other Colors. Ask me for a Color, and I'll tell you their ability. The Legend is longer. I'll tell you that once we go home to Haven.*

Ray sighed. **Yellow,** she said, thinking of the water-bearer, Karylla.

Endless energy, Laenyn replied. *A Silk Yellow needs only one night of sleep in a week to feel refreshed, I have been told.*

What do they do with all that extra time? Ray asked, thinking of the long tracts of time they must spend at home, waiting for the dawn. Laenyn shrugged, and Ray moved on. **What about Red?** Ray asked, knowing that they sat between the Blues and the Yellows.

Intelligence, Laenyn replied. *An uncanny way of looking at numbers and knowing how they fit. With a village as small as Ilonon, maximizing our numbers is important. I don't understand the specific applications or uses, but that's what I was taught.*

Yellow's got energy. Red's got smarts. Ray nodded, trying to get herself to remember. **Okay, I think I've got it. What about —**

Ray heard something in the distance, and her thoughts broke off. Suddenly, she realized that there was another scent in the air, something that made her breath catch.

"Smoke," Laenyn whispered aloud. Getting to her feet, she returned to the clearing. The other Keshaan stood in precise lines, but Laenyn was the only Green Keshaan. Lady Dayan stood at the front of the group.

"We will drive the beast from Ilonon, whatever it may be," Lady Dayan said, her voice sharp and loud. Something crashed in the distance, and Ray could hear pale threads of screams from the other side of town. "The beast has entered from the Cotton side, near Lake Anonwe. Any cowardice will be punished with death. Go!"

CHAPTER SEVENTEEN

The women dispersed, and Laenyn took off, her breaths burning her throat with the raw, cold air. Fright pulsed through her veins, making her grip on her staff weak as her fingers trembled beyond her control. A fight. Her first fight.

What are we fighting? Ray asked. Laenyn darted through the Main Hall to get to the Cotton side faster.

It doesn't matter, Laenyn replied, mouth dry as she darted around tables and benches. The other Keshaan were already ahead of her; she heard shattering and screaming at the far end of the room, behind the door that hid the Council's chamber, but a metallic shriek drowned it out. *This is my chance. If I succeed, then I become a full-fledged Keshaan.*

Laenyn burst through the other doorway, and the earth trembled beneath their feet. Ray watched as Laenyn looked up, and up—a mass of black scales towered above them, taller than any building. Ray remembered Laenyn's words as she'd drifted off on the field—a snake-like monster too enormous to fully comprehend. A monster that decimated villages.

A Haubonalyr, Laenyn gasped, nearly dropping her staff.

Ray noticed the other Keshaan quailing, all of them staring, transfixed, at the beast's tail. Laenyn followed their gaze, and Ray gasped. Three long, snake-like tails flared around the Haubona-lyr, each long enough to reach its mouth. As Ray watched, the Haubonalyr struck down a fleeing wolf with one of the bony, scythe-like protrusions on its tail. The wolf howled and became a little girl in a black dress. She was limp as a doll when it tore off her arm. Laenyn looked away, gulping.

I have to fight it.

Oh, no, you don't! That thing will kill us! It's got three tails, Laenyn! That's not right!

Three tails, each with three, poisoned scythes. Three fins, each strong enough to crush a building and everyone inside it. Three eyes that see in any darkness, that can focus with such precision that they seldom miss their target. Its scales are nearly invulnerable.

How is that supposed to reassure me?

It's better to go into the battle knowing what you're fighting, Laenyn said. *If we flee, we will be killed for our cowardice. If we can drive it out of the village, then I will be a Keshaan in full, at long last free of my apprenticeship.*

Ray balked as Laenyn began to run forward. A Keshaan in a blue dress lay on the ground; Ray realized, with sickening horror, that only the upper half of her body remained, her face twisted in the agony of death. Too horrified to scream, Ray lost control of the body to Laenyn.

Laenyn ran through the pooling blood, staining their dress. The dizziness threatened to overwhelm them both; she felt Laenyn suppress a gag as the warmth of the blood soaked into their shoes. Laenyn didn't hesitate, constantly switching direction and rolling to the side as one of the Haubonalyr's tails struck at the ground beside her. The bony scythe was as long as Laenyn was tall, and Ray saw their face reflected in its poisonous sheen— a expression both determined and strong, with eyes that were wild with terror.

The Haubonalyr cried—a loud, piercing shriek that made their ears ring and set the world spinning. The ground seemed above their heads, but Laenyn kept running. Another woman screamed as she fell and was caught; Ray saw a spray of yellow blood splatter against the ground.

Slowly, the Haubonalyr moved forward, its fin striking down a building to their right. The Haubonalyr moved another fin forward, and Ray heard a child's wail that was swallowed in the resulting crash. A bolt of vivid, red lightning struck the fin on its back.

Energy-magic.

Laenyn tensed, swallowing hard as she dove to one side. The Haubonalyr's scythe caught the hem of her dress, tearing it and sending her sprawling in the wrong direction. Laenyn cried out as she leapt from the ground to her feet, brandishing her staff. It ignited with green fire, making the Haubonalyr hesitate long enough for her to dart away, hiding beneath its bulk, where it was said to be the most vulnerable.

If you take energy out of it, it'll age!

We're not even sure we can make that work properly on a flower!

The mass of black scales above her suddenly shifted forward, and Laenyn's heart felt as thought it would burst in their chest. She dodged to one side, turning it into a diving roll as she tripped over the corpse of the woman who had mocked her on her first day as a Keshaan apprentice. The Haubonalyr slammed downward, sending her flying as the ground gave a concussive burst. Laenyn's ears rang, and she saw double for an instant—long enough to be skewered, if Dayan hadn't taken that opportunity to zap the Haubonalyr with a bolt of her own energy. Dayan breathed heavily, looking five years older, and Laenyn looked away.

They're not doing a damn thing! Ray screamed. The Haubonalyr twitched as another bolt of life energy struck it, looking younger and more lively than before. It hardly looked more bothered than a person plagued by flies. **We have to at least try,**

Laenyn!

Ray felt half mad. Laenyn's gaze treated the corpses as obstacles, not registering the madly swirling bloodstains as the colors ran and mixed, not understanding that there were children screaming for their mothers, only to be eaten alive. Laenyn stepped around a half-chewed head that had been spat out, leaving little more than a gaping skull. Ray wanted to vomit—she screamed instead.

We can't stop it! Ray was desperate, but she could feel Laenyn's cold, calm mind. **What do you think we can do?**

It's honorable to die in battle, at least, Laenyn said, her voice like ice water. *There's nothing we can do, Ray; Haubonalyrs only leave when they've eaten their fill!*

Laenyn ran alongside a nearby house, winded and sore. Her cheek was bleeding, as were the knuckles on the hand that held her staff. A cursory glance told her that no fewer than ten of the Keshaan had been killed. The Haubonalyr seemed to be picky about which parts of them it ate; it invariably spat out the cloaks, leaving nothing more than the torn, stained cloth. Sometimes it would spit out large bones; Laenyn dodged to one side as it dropped a femur, and tripped over the severed head from before. Laenyn looked into its dangling, bloody eyes. She could see the chipped bone through a ragged gash in its cheek; it was sticky with red blood.

Laenyn! Ray screamed. The Haubonalyr's tail flared; fewer bolts were striking it. **You have to move!** Laenyn rolled onto her back and looked up at the sky. The Haubonalyr looked back at her, eyes red and keen with intelligence. It could see that she was giving up. Ray fought to take control. **This is your chance to prove yourself!** Ray howled. **Get up and fight, or let me fight it off myself!**

Laenyn rolled onto her side as the Haubonalyr's tail surged forward. Beside her stood Lady Dayan, who looked twenty years older than she had that morning; she had almost no energy-magic left to give. For an instant, she met Laenyn's eyes and smiled.

Then she was dust on the wind, and the Haubonalyr was howling as it waved its singed and bleeding tail. Laenyn couldn't comprehend it—she couldn't imagine Ilonon without Lady Dayan. To age herself to the point of death—

"No!" Laenyn screamed, forcing herself to her feet to face the Haubonalyr.

I can't do this alone.

Ray moved immediately, their steps falling in sync. There was an energy in working together that Ray had never known before—their very skin seemed to prickle and vibrate. Raising their staff as one, they cried out together. Fury crackled in the air around them, a dark, sparkling green.

They swept their staff, feeling for the life that pulsed through the Haubonalyr's body—its heartbeat was slow and unconcerned. Tugging on the staff, they hauled out some of the Haubonalyr's energy. It glittered, vibrant, above the Haubonalyr's head.

Together, they yanked again, and more energy joined the crackling thundercloud above the Haubonalyr. It was older than before—older than it had been at the start of battle. Adrenaline pounded and throbbed in their ears, making their hands shake with the tension and energy of battle.

Stepping forward, they cried out, swinging the staff. The energy spiked downward; just as the grass had caught fire when they'd tried to feed it its own energy, the Haubonalyr screamed in agony as its scales smoldered.

They drew the staff upward in a sharp arc before leaping forward to slam it against the earth. Energy tore itself free of the Haubonalyr, aging it again, and then crashed inward again—it was ablaze and floundering with hideous screams of pain.

It slumped to the ground to roll and put out the flames, but they anticipated it; they struck one last time, drawing out more energy than either previous time. It wailed, and, sweeping their staff against the dusty, bloodstained earth, they curved the energy away from the Haubonalyr, spiking it into the ground at its feet.

The fire went out, and black smoke swept over the battle-field. They gagged on the air, which was thick with the taste of burnt flesh. Finally, the dust cleared, leaving only a gaping, black stain in the soil that reeked of death and decay, as well as a long trail of destruction. They looked around, numb.

The silence hung in the air, and they sank to their knees, pride flooding their chest. The rank stench of the Haubonalyr and the gutted corpses brought them out of their glowing daze, and their smile fell a little. There was a chill behind the heat of exertion and battle; the fires had been quenched.

They looked down at their bloodstained hands, which were sticky with blue and red blood. With that, the spell seemed to break—Ray was Ray, and Laenyn was Laenyn, and they could never be whole again.

CHAPTER EIGHTEEN

Ray felt like there was a hole in her chest; Laenyn felt numb with disbelief and confusion.

"Lady Dayan would have been proud, Laenyn," a young woman in black silk said. Her hair was not yet dyed; Laenyn remembered that she was going to be fifteen in the spring, but had been allowed an apprenticeship early.

"Thank you, Miss Cyna," Laenyn replied. "Please excuse me, but I must check for survivors in the damaged buildings."

"Of course," Cyna replied. "Your house may have been damaged, after all. Is your daughter still at home?"

Mother! Laenyn said sharply. Ray jumped.

What's the matter? Ray asked. **Isn't she at the lake?**

They beat her for stealing the food for Haven, Laenyn said. *After you pulled back. They ordered her to stay home today!*

"Perhaps," Laenyn said. "I think that we should each check our own Color. The ket-amen will be here soon to check the bodies of the other Keshaan. Pardon me."

Laenyn bowed and strode off, breaking into a run as she passed the first ruined building.

What about Haven?

The elation that Ray had felt after slaying the Haubonalyr had vanished; their heart hammered in their chest. For the most part, the Haubonalyr had taken the path between the houses, but it had been too wide to get by without damaging some houses on each side of the road. Ray saw a house in the Purple row ahead that had been completely leveled where the Haubonalyr's path had swerved.

She should be at home with Mother, Laenyn answered. Their home was along the path from the forest—Laenyn's eyes fixed on it, and some of the anxiety unknotted in her chest. It was whole and intact.

As long as they didn't go outside to see what the commotion was, Laenyn prayed. She'd lectured Wylwon about it before, after beginning her apprenticeship. Had she listened? She'd never thought to warn Haven.

Laenyn leapt up all four stairs leading up to her porch and flung the paper door to the side. Empty.

"Mother!" Laenyn shouted, not shutting the door behind her, not caring that anyone on the street could hear her. "Haven!"

The closet door slid open immediately; Haven darted out and flung her arms around Laenyn's legs. Behind her, Wylwon staggered out of the closet, her face streaked with tears.

"Laenyn," Wylwon said haltingly, leaning on the door for support. "But—the Haubonalyr—"

"I slew it," Laenyn said.

We slew it.

"Then you'll no longer be an apprentice," Wylwon said. Her eyes filled with tears, and she stumbled forward, dragging Laenyn and Haven alike into a fierce hug. "Oh, stars, I thought that I'd lost you."

"You haven't," Laenyn said, but Ray could tell that she didn't know how to react to the sudden outpouring of sentiment.

"Why, Laenyn?" Wylwon sobbed, burying her face in Laenyn's shoulder. "Why did you choose to become a Keshaan? I just want you to be safe!"

"I keep us safe!" Laenyn's distress seeped into Ray. "What do you think would have happened if I hadn't been there, Mother?"

"They are blessed to have such a protector," Wylwon said. "And I am likewise blessed to have such a resolute and well-behaved daughter."

She's just worried about you, Laenyn.

She's a scientist, Ray—they're despised by the Council. Only inventors are more loathed. She's too soft—she's too disobedient—if I hadn't become a Keshaan—

"You are all that I have," Wylwon said, pulling back to cup Laenyn's face. "I don't mean to sound ungrateful. I know how much you have sacrificed. Just once—just *once*—I wish that I could protect you, instead."

Ray felt tears welling up in their eyes.

"Stay safe," Laenyn answered, pulling Wylwon back into her arms. "That's all I ask, Mother. Please."

Octavia Thyn

CHAPTER NINETEEN

Ray was quiet while Laenyn examined the Secondaries' houses for casualties. The Primaries were invested in their own rows and couldn't be bothered. It was numbing labor, examining rubble for corpses or injured women, and Laenyn moved with a keen, detached efficiency.

The final tally was thirty-two deaths and six injuries in the Secondaries' rows. Most women had been away at work. Twenty-eight of the casualties were their daughters, who had been forced to wait at home. Sawyn was among the dead.

Finally, the surviving Keshaan gathered in their training field; the sky faded above them, bringing nightfall. Dayan's daughter, Kevair, stood before the group. Though her face was a mask of stoicism, the twilight couldn't quite hide the tear tracks on her face. Laenyn knew that she was eighteen, and had been an apprentice that morning. She looked much older, now.

"My mother sacrificed herself to slay the Haubonalyr," Kevair said. "The only Secondary in a decade that was permitted to become a Keshaan, and only at my mother's behest, finished her work. We all fought today, and in three days' time, there will be a ceremony to grant all apprentices full power and authority as Keshaan. This will bring with it great responsibility. Ordinarily, I would tell you all that we will be swearing fealty to the Council on that day."

Kevair paused, and Ray noticed the tension in her eyes. The woman who had conducted exercises stepped forward, her face imperious, and Kevair stepped down.

What's going on? Ray asked. Laenyn shushed her.

That's Devolair, Laenyn replied. *Araya Devolair Miria Senea Thyn's eldest daughter.*

"I regret to inform you that there was a rebellion not thirty feet from you while you fought the Haubonalyr," Devolair said. Her voice was high and piercing.

A rebellion?

Laenyn silenced her immediately.

"My mother grew weak in her old age," Devolair said. "She saw enemies everywhere, and imagined that they surrounded her. For that reason, and the honeyed lies of a Lower, she was driven to the verge of insanity. Today, as the world seemed to be falling apart around her, she attacked the other Council members."

A collective gasp came from the crowd; there was no hiding the shock in any face, no matter how weary.

"*Your* Council member got away with only a few scratches," Devolair said, eyeing Laenyn. Laenyn quickly shut her mouth and knelt at attention, hiding the exhaustion in her posture. "However, no Primary Council member survived unscathed, and the Orange and White members were murdered. The Pink one escaped mostly unharmed, as well. However, in three days' time, they will all be put to death, barring further crises."

Kevair spoke when Devolair gave her a pointed look, but her voice was a little shaky. "Until then, as is customary for the murder of a Haubonalyr, every Keshaan who participated in the fight will fast. At our initiation ceremony, apprentices will execute all traitors."

No one spoke; the silence hung in the air.

"The names of those that have been condemned by the Grand Council Woman, Devolair Cyna Octavia Thyn, are as follows: Araya, Maria, Saren, Anon, Alia, Notten, Glensa, Onni, Alena. They do not deserve recognition for their Colors, as they have deviated from the natural order of things. They are henceforth stripped of all but their given names."

"Yes?" Kevair asked, pointing at a woman behind Laenyn. "I believe that you had a question."

"In what manner shall we put them to death, my lady?" the woman asked. Kevair's face stiffened, but she turned respectfully toward Lady Devolair.

"The knife," Devolair replied. "Their blood shall be drained and their bodies buried. This is the punishment that traitors deserve."

"Yes, my lady," they chorused. Laenyn's tongue fumbled for speech, even with the automatic reply.

"For now, you are dismissed," she said, waving her hand. "All of you should return to your homes and meditate. Unless you are required to rebuild a home," Devolair looked pointedly at Laenyn, whose face burned; she was the only Cotton Keshaan, and no one else had had family to worry about. "I expect you all to remain totally indoors, thinking about the enormity of the responsibility that approaches. Good evening. I will see your families at dinner, assuming that they survived."

"Good evening, Grand Council Woman," they chorused. Laenyn felt dizzy and sick.

That was not what I was expecting, she whispered, bowing enough to press her head against the dirt before standing. Araya's face appeared in her mind, commanding and omnipotent. *No one could kill her. No one.*

Why do we have to kill anyone? Ray demanded. **I don't want anyone's blood on my hands!**

We'll probably be asked to kill the Green Council Woman, Anon. Laenyn walked home in a daze. Ray looked around on her behalf, trying to stay alert. As they passed the ruined houses, women with crude tools in their hands glanced at them. Laenyn dragged their staff, trudging forward—with their disapproving gazes, Ray brought up their posture and held their staff upright. There was enough to worry about without fearing whatever punishment Ilonon might have for slouching.

Laenyn, I don't know what's going on! I barely know anything about the Colors—you told me that Red was smart, and Yellow had endless energy, but I still don't know the rest.

We'll have plenty of time to think over the next three days, Laenyn murmured. *Time to prepare ourselves. We wouldn't be asked to kill Araya; we're the Lowest of the Keshaan.* Something eased in Laenyn's chest. Ray felt frustration building up in her own; their heart struggled to follow the both of them until Ray relinquished control over it.

I don't know anything! Ray shouted. The fury was sudden and foreign—that old anger, the kind that came from nowhere she knew. **I haven't spoken to Haven since you got back! You haven't really explained things to me—it's like I'm looking at half the pieces to a puzzle, but everyone's trying to keep me from seeing the whole picture at once!**

Please, Ray, Laenyn murmured. Her voice was weary and overburdened; Ray suddenly knew that Laenyn was past the point of being able to handle another attack. *This isn't the time.*

Ray sank. She couldn't stay angry at Laenyn when she took that tone. Resigning herself to further waiting, she slid the door open and stepped inside. Haven was waiting, excitement bright on her face, but her expression fell as she met Ray's eyes. Ray stepped into the closet, feeling too exposed in the open air of the main room of the house. Wylwon was there, wringing her hands. When she saw Ray, she opened her mouth, but Ray shook her head and Wylwon fell silent.

Dimly, she realized that Laenyn had drifted off to sleep; their mind was quiet. Sinking back against the wall, Ray closed her eyes, pressing her forehead against her knees.

"What's the matter?" Wylwon asked. "Are you all right?"

"It's been a long day," Ray murmured. Now that she'd stopped moving around so much, exhaustion fell like a curtain over her. "I used a lot of energy." Of course, the energy-magic. Ray remembered how exhausted she'd been after trying the stunt with the flower. The floor fell like a chasm at her feet. Her heart slowed, her breathing evened, and her eyes fluttered. "I think I..." Ray began, her body slipping to one side.

"Laenyn!" Wylwon shouted, diving to catch her.

Ray was out before she hit the floor.

Renee Marie Marsh
(Ray)

CHAPTER TWENTY

Ray woke in her own loft, when the room was dark and the world was silent. Laenyn still slept, but Haven tossed and turned at her side. Ray rubbed her shoulder to ease her fears, and Haven snapped awake with a gasp.

"M-mommy?" Haven whispered. Ray thought of Dayan reaching into Laenyn's head, the constant listening. Better to whisper, too. Better to make it a habit to keep quiet.

"No, I'm Ray," Ray yawned, dragging herself to a sitting position. Haven looked at her warily.

"Is Mommy around?" Haven asked. Her voice was tight with fear.

"She's asleep," Ray replied. "You haven't talked to me since she got back, Haven. It's okay. I'm your big sister; I'm supposed to listen to your nightmares, right?" **Not that I remember doing that in Phoenix,** Ray admitted to herself. **I don't remember much of anything.**

"You can't be Ray," Haven said, shaking her head. "You don't make any sense."

"I'm Ray," Ray insisted, getting off the uncomfortable pile of straw to lie where the wall bent into the ceiling. The enclosed space was comforting—she felt hidden and safe. "Just talk to me,

Haven. I just want to know what's going on, and Laenyn won't tell me all the Colors, or explain what the Legend is, or tell me who the Council was, or even tell me what our job is as a Ke-shaan. I know that she knows more than she's willing to tell me, but I don't know why she's hiding it from me!"

Ray turned to look at Haven, whose face was masked by shadows. After a long pause, Haven got off the mattress and scooted over to Ray, looking down at her as she lay on the floor.

"You're not angry enough to be Ray," Haven said. "That's all I remember about Ray, really: she was angry, and angry at me most of all. Even when I baited you to bring out Mommy, you didn't try to hit me."

Ray sat up so sharply that she banged her head. The sound wasn't loud enough to wake Wylwon, who continued snoring from the other loft. Ray's head rang, and words leapt up before her, falling like shadows in her mind: If you want me to hit you, fine! I'll hit you so hard that you'll scream!

"I don't want to be angry," Ray said. "Why would I hit you?" She curled sideways, rubbing her head and ignoring the frighten-ing anger that lurked like a demon in her heart. "I don't want anyone's blood on my hands." Ray looked down at her bloody, unwashed hands as she gave up on soothing her head. "I don't want anyone's pain on my conscience."

"Then you're not Ray," Haven said. "You can't be."

The burning fury looked Ray in the eye in their mind space. It looked like a specter, like a nightmare—it was smoke and shad-ow with fire for eyes and blood pooling at its feet; its grin was sharp as a blade.

Maybe the reason that you don't remember anything is be-cause I'm the real Ray, she hissed in Ray's ear. Ray shuddered.

I am Ray! Ray replied. **I know I am!**

"Ray?" Haven's whisper broke the spell. Ray heard herself sniffling. "Why are you crying?"

"I don't have anything else to hold on to," Ray said. "If I'm not Ray, then I don't know who I am. Haven, what happened to me? Why did you leave Phoenix?"

Haven shook her head. "I've never even told Mommy that story. It's too dangerous. I can't tell anyone the truth."

"Why?" Ray asked. "Why did you hate me when I first came here? Was I mean to you in Phoenix?"

"You hated me," Haven said, looking at the ground. "You hated me more than anyone, I think. You said that I ruined your family. I'm glad you've forgotten why. I—you have to understand, Ray. There are some memories that hurt to think about. There are some memories that make life harder, that make everything scarier and riskier and deadlier. Especially in Ilonon."

Ray rolled onto her back, staring at the ceiling that angled inches above her face.

"How long ago did you live in Phoenix?" Ray asked. "Can you at least tell me how much time I've lost?"

"I don't know the answer, Ray," Haven replied. "I lost track of time. Maybe two years? It's so hard to explain—I don't think I can tell you anything about the past."

Ray nodded, too tired to pursue it. The sky was tinged with gold, and her stomach growled. Her mouth was grimy, and her hands were covered in dried, flaking blood.

"Can you at least tell me about the Colors?" Ray asked. "Laenyn told me about Green, Blue, Purple, Yellow, Red, and Black. I guess that's a pretty good number; I don't know. There are more that I don't know, though. Please, Haven. Can't you at least tell me about that?"

"I'll tell you the Legend after breakfast, if Mommy won't. I have nothing else to do today." Haven sighed heavily. "I still don't understand why you don't know anything about Colors; you were a Pure Blue, and you loved it." Haven shook her head. "Okay. I'll tell you the Colors. Just tell me the ones that you don't know."

"I guess I'll try to fill in the holes in the rainbow first," Ray sighed. "I know Red already. What about Orange?"

"That's a pretty cool one," Haven smiled. "Orange people can make fire with their minds."

"Wow!" Ray said, turning on one elbow to look at Haven. "Just by thinking about it?"

Haven nodded. "It's like energy-magic, I think," she said. "Mommy told me a little bit about that, and you can make fires, so I'm pretty sure that it's not so different."

"Huh," Ray said, lying back down. "I wonder why none of them are Keshaan, then."

"The Legend explains the ranking system," Haven said. "I don't want to get into all the ranks and Uppers and Lowers until you know about the Legend."

"Fine," Ray agreed. "So I know Red, Orange, Yellow, Green, Blue, and Purple. I guess that takes care of the rainbow. What other Colors are there?"

"Black, White, Gray, Brown, and Pink," Haven answered.

"I know Black," Ray nodded. She thought of Jauge, with her cat-like eyes, and the row of people with bright, white hair. "What about White?"

"They can see in the dark," Haven said. "They see as clearly by moonlight as by daylight. Also, they're usually more... What's the word? Free-spirited? Adaptable? Creative? It's been so long since I spoke English. There's no word for it in Yra, that's for sure."

"That seems like it'd be useful," Ray said. "You're a better speaker than most kids your age, I think."

"It's nothing special," Haven said, looking away. "Not for me, anyway."

"What about the last three?" Ray asked. "I didn't know that Pink would be a Color." She remembered the women dressed in pink only after speaking. "Why is it that White and Red make a specific Color, but Blue and White don't?"

"Blue was too Pure to submit to White," Haven replied in Yra, her tone carefully practiced. She shook her head. "It doesn't matter. Pinks take their creativity from White and their intelligence from Red. Their ability is to speak any language at all. They can speak it perfectly, too, once they've heard enough words to get a pattern together."

"That would be great," Ray sighed. "You could talk to any-one."

"It's useless in Ilonon," Haven muttered, and Ray sighed again, less wistfully.

"Yeah, I guess so," Ray closed her eyes. "So Orange people can make fire, White people can see in the dark, and Pink people can speak any language. What about Brown and Gray?"

"They work together in the fields," Haven replied. "Grays get the ability to get plants to grow. The purest Grays can grow a tree all the way in just one night, if the weather is right and the soil is good. That's where the Browns come in: they can control the weather." Ray looked at her skeptically, and Haven shrugged. "That's how Ilonon manages to keep everyone fed, even though it's so small and doesn't trade with anyone. I don't know why you'd believe a woman could turn herself into an animal, but wouldn't believe another one could make a cloud or make it rain."

"Point taken," Ray said. She let out a long breath. "So I used to be psychic?"

"Yeah," Haven said. Something about this bothered Ray, but the dawn was coming and her eyelids felt heavy.

"Thanks, Haven," Ray said. "I'm glad that someone finally ex-plained things to me."

"I'll tell you about the Legend later," Haven said, taking Ray by the arm. "Come on, we have to get to breakfast."

Ray shook her head. "Laenyn is supposed to be fasting. We can't leave the house for three days." Haven's eyes went wide.

"You're going to be really hungry and irritable by the end of the third day," she muttered. "I guess that I'll go get Wylwon. I'll be back after breakfast, then."

"Yeah, thanks," Ray yawned, curling so that her face was in shadow. "I'll be here, just waiting. It's okay to wake me up."

"Okay," Haven said. "I'm sorry that I was so mean to you when you first got here, Ray. I didn't know—I didn't know that you'd be like this."

"That's okay," Ray said, closing her eyes and drifting off to sleep. "You just wanted your mommy. There's not much I can do about that. G'night, Haven."

"Good night," Haven answered. Her voice was distant and sad as she pulled away, but Ray was too far gone to respond.

CHAPTER TWENTY-ONE

Ray woke to the sound of Laenyn's voice. Looking around, she saw that they were already in the closet; she smelled sawdust in the air, and noticed that the light pouring through the window was green.

"If another Haubonalyr attacks someday, stay inside," Laenyn instructed Haven, who watched with an attentive expression on her face. "Even if it makes it as far as the house, you're more likely to survive a collapsed roof than the Haubonalyr's poison." Sawyn had been injured from the beating, hadn't received food for a day and a half. They'd found her under a pile of rubble, neck snapped. Less painful, maybe, but Ray's gut still constricted. Laenyn flinched at the image. "I want you to stay safe, Haven."

Haven looked away at the window for a moment as she nodded, saying, "Of course, Mommy."

Haven promised she'd tell me the Legend. Ray yawned, not ready to think about what lay ahead of them, not ready to comprehend what it meant to put someone to death. That Legend seemed like the key to understanding Ilonon—she needed somewhere to start.

She has it memorized already? Laenyn replied, surprised. "Haven," she said aloud. Haven looked at her, startled out of her reverie. "Ray just told me that you promised to tell her the Legend. I didn't know that you had it all memorized, since you've only been here for a year."

"I've been practicing," Haven admitted, blushing. "There's nothing else to do all day but sit and think. I don't have all the details memorized, though. Will you explain if I mess up?"

Laenyn nodded, and Ray took over.

"Go on," Ray said, leaning forward to rest her elbows on her knees. "I'm listening."

"Okay," Haven began, smoothing her skirt as she settled against the wall. "Long, long ago, there was nothingness. Out of the nothingness came two Colors: Black and White. They lived side by side for ages without argument, but eventually White started to think that he was better than Black. He called himself the first born, even though he was no older than Black, and started calling Black names."

Are we talking about people here, or—

Shh.

"Black realized that White planned to overthrow her and make her obey him, so she made the Primary Colors: Blue, Red, and Yellow," Haven closed her eyes, ticking off her fingers as she listed them. "Blue could listen to White's thoughts and figure out when he would attack, Red could form a battle plan, and Yellow had the energy to pull through the fight."

Haven nodded once to herself, then glanced at Ray.

Tell her that she's doing fine.

"Laenyn says you're doing great," Ray said. "Go on."

Haven nodded, and continued, "White wasn't strong enough to make his own troops, so he forced Black's troops together, making," Haven's brow furrowed, and she muttered under her breath in English, "Shoot, Brown came later, with Gray. First was..." Haven shut her eyes, ticking off her fingers. "No, no, first he tried to mix himself with each of Black's Guards, but only Pink survived." Haven sighed. "*Then* he mixed together Red and Yellow, but Orange was born feet first and deformed."

Orange women have large feet, Laenyn explained.

Way to ignore the fact that they can manipulate fire, Ray grumbled.

"The next to be born was Green, who multiplied too quickly and didn't get along well with the others. Finally, White made Purple, who used Blue's psychic powers and Red's intelligence well, making it the most normal of the Secondaries."

So White is 'he', Black is 'she', and we are 'it'. Great.

Haven looked at Ray, biting her lip, and Ray waved a hand at her to get her to continue. Nodding slowly, Haven began again.

"White wasn't happy with his army," Haven said.

When he had a soldier that was hard to kill, a soldier that could make fire, and a soldier that could levitate stuff? Poor baby.

"So he decided to mix all of Black's Guards together to make Brown. Brown was so powerful that it was like a creator itself, controlling the heavens," Haven stumbled, biting her lip again. "And... Then... Right! Brown wouldn't stand for being controlled by White, so White made a last, desperate attempt to get the power he'd been aiming for: he mixed himself together with Black, making Gray, who also refused to follow him."

"So what happened to the war?" Ray asked, after a long silence. Haven shook herself.

"What?" she asked, blinking. "Oh, right. The Secondaries weren't men or women, so they didn't know who to follow, but Brown and Gray sided with Black and the Primaries, and the other Secondaries followed. White was banished to the Underground Caverns, and all men must follow him." Haven frowned. "How was that, Mommy? Did I get it all right?"

"You did a wonderful job," Laenyn said, taking control for a moment.

"Was that helpful, Ray?" Haven asked, cocking her head to one side. "It explains why the order goes Black, Blue, Red, Yellow, Gray, Brown, Purple, Green, Orange, Pink, White."

"As though I can follow a list like that," Ray laughed. "Yeah, I guess it helped. It helped me figure out that people in Ilonon are as crazy as I thought they were."

It's our history, Laenyn said. Her voice carried the weight of a society. *That's why men are sent Below and hybrids must be killed. Men are born traitors, and hybrids are a corruption of what little Purity Black was able to leave intact after White's insurrection.*

You're nuts, Ray said flatly. **An old story doesn't justify murder. An old story doesn't justify denying other people rights.**

It's more than an old story! Laenyn said, her voice sharp. *It's the Truth; it tells us how to live, how to conduct ourselves, what is forbidden—Haven left out the details, but it forms the foundation of our society.*

Prejudice is sure a great foundation to build on, isn't it? Ray snapped. The anger surged up again; in her mind's eye, she saw it lurking behind Laenyn, waiting to strike. Ray swallowed. **This isn't right, Laenyn. None of it is.**

Il o non, Laenyn whispered, almost laughing. Sadness touched Laenyn, dispelling the rage-filled ghast. *Peace by Separation. How can we live without that separation, Ray? Iltyplyam is our greeting: Il ty Plyam. Peace for Betters. The word for mother is almost identical to the word for Better. In all ways of thought, the Primaries are held above us, and mixing is treated as the most foul abomination. How can we live without that?*

I'm living without it.

You weren't raised here.

You could pick up and leave Ilonon right this minute— take Wylwon and Haven with you and run. They don't have any real power over you.

Ludicrous! Fear knotted, icy, in Laenyn's chest, so potent that it spilled over into Ray. *That's—Ray, you have no idea what power they hold! If we did something half so foolish as running and got caught, we would be put to death.*

They're going to make us murder someone, Laenyn! Ray shouted. Haven watched them with horror-stricken eyes; Ray turned away. **I can't do it. I can't kill someone, no matter what kind of a person they are. I don't want to live in this awful place any more! I want to go home!**

I, I, I, I! Laenyn snapped. *I can't, I can't, I don't, I want! Can you even hear yourself?*

Doesn't it bother you at *all***?** Ray demanded. **I—why should we have to kill anyone, Laenyn?**

It's a Keshaan's job to put enemies of Ilonon to death, Laenyn said, pulling away from Ray. *They aren't human; they aren't tied to a Family or Color any more.*

I can't talk to you right now, Ray said, the shadow of rage falling over her again. **Right now, Laenyn, you're sickening me.**

"Sorry about that, Haven," Ray said quietly. "Laenyn and I were kind of having an argument."

"I heard," Haven said, shaking. Ray looked at her sharply, and she drew back against the wall. "Oh, uh, you started talking, uh, out loud for some of it."

"We'll have to be careful about that, I guess," Ray sighed, slumping backwards to fall on her back and stare up at the ceiling. Her stomach whined loudly, making her blush. "This is going to be a long three days."

"Yeah," Haven said. "At least I'll get to see Mommy more often."

"Do you really just stay home alone all the time?" Ray asked. Haven nodded. "For all those hours that we have to practice on the field?" Haven nodded again, and Ray let out a long, low whistle. "The least I can do is give you something to practice."

"What do you mean, Ray?" Haven asked, licking her lips. Ray pushed herself to a sitting position, trying to distract herself with anything but Laenyn and her own fury. She didn't want to hurt anyone! Laenyn went off in a huff.

I'm going to sleep, she announced.

"I'm going to show you how to use energy-magic!" Ray said, looking around for her staff. It had rolled into a nearby corner when she'd fallen asleep the day before. Seeing it, Ray moved to grab it.

"What?" Haven said, plainly shocked. "Mommy may have explained a little bit of it to me, but she never—" Haven shook her head as Ray sat up, staff in hand.

You can't, Ray. You barely understand it yourself.

I'm the one who thought of the new idea, Ray said, testing the weight of the staff in her hand. **If I hadn't, we wouldn't have killed the Haubonalyr. Now, come on.**

No! Laenyn shouted. *It's completely forbidden to teach magic to anyone who—*

"Do you want to learn?" Ray asked, leaning forward. Some time before Ray had woken up, Laenyn must have cleaned off— there was no more dried blood clinging to her hands and dress. "Laenyn tells me that I'm not supposed to, but I'm kind of sick of all these rules, you know?"

"Well, if Mommy..." Haven began, licking her lips again. "If it's against the rules, then I can't exactly..."

"Who's going to know?" Ray asked. Haven gave her an exasperated look, and Ray shrugged. "I know, there are Blues who can read minds. Don't think about it when you're around them. You're home alone most of the day, right?" Haven nodded hesitantly, and Ray lifted her staff with a firm nod. "See? I bet that you could get pretty good at it if you practiced."

"I... I guess so," Haven murmured.

"No, Haven," Laenyn said, wresting over control of their mouth. "It's too dangerous. I won't allow it."

Ray felt Laenyn's exhaustion eating away at her. She knew that Laenyn would shut her out of control completely if she had the power to do it. It was the first time that Ray had held more control over the body than Laenyn, and it felt heady.

"She says it's dangerous," Ray said, taking back control. "But I think that's up to you to decide."

"I'm only six," Haven murmured, looking away. "I should listen to Mommy. We can do something else."

Ray sighed. "All right," she said. She leaned back against the closet wall. "But think about it, okay?"

"I will," Haven said. Her voice was soft and far away as she watched the window pane. "I have a lot of time for thinking."

Silence fell, awkward and thick. Ray set the staff down, and it clattered away, rolling against the wall with a thunk. Haven winced.

"You don't want to tell me anything about Phoenix," Ray said, not meeting Haven's eyes. "Can you even tell me why?"

"I don't want to do anything that could bring back the old Ray," Haven said. "You don't remember why you hated me, but if you knew..." Haven sighed, shaking her head. Her shoulders sank as though she was bearing an enormous weight on them, and she rested her chin on her palms. "I don't know, Ray. It's so hard to think of you as 'Ray,' since you're so different. But if you really are Ray, and I give you back that reason to hurt me, I— I don't know what I'd do if the real Ray came back."

Ray snorted and tossed her head backward, banging it on the wall behind her; her head rang, and two Havens ghosted in front of her before she blinked them away. Embarrassed, Ray drew her knees up against her chest and pressed her forehead against them.

"I am the real Ray," Ray whispered, blocking out the rage that hovered just out of sight, like a ghost. It made anger flicker in her chest to look at it; it was darker and more tangible than it had been before. I am the real Ray, it mouthed back at her, mocking her with a silent laugh. Ray covered her ears, willing it away. "I am the real Ray."

"Okay, okay," Haven said quickly. When Ray looked up, Haven was watching her with eyes that shone with curiosity. She felt like an animal on display. "I won't say it again," Haven said, her voice softer. "I just—I remember a very different Ray."

"Right," Ray murmured. "It's okay."

Ray noticed that Laenyn had been silent for a while; it took another moment to find her, fast asleep in a dingy corner of their mind.

"Your mommy's asleep," Ray said. The air felt tinged with a distant chill—the window paper had darkened to teal. "I just don't know if I'm ever going to understand Ilonon. What's the point of all the beatings, for one thing? Sawyn didn't even do anything wrong, and..." Ray shook her head. Haven's eyes caught the slanted light, glowing a brilliant green as they shifted. "But what I *really* can't understand is how they treat men and so-called hybrids." Ray smacked her palm against the floor. "Laenyn is totally brainwashed! She thinks it's okay to kill hybrids." Haven's eyes went wide, and she swallowed audibly. Ray covered her face again. "She thinks it's fair to send men to live underground their whole lives. I don't—I can't—understand it. It's *wrong*. It makes me sick to my stomach with—I don't even know. It makes me angry and disgusted and I can't figure out how to change her mind." Ray dug her fingers into the rough cloth of her dress, clenching her teeth. "I want to get the hell out of Ilonon, Haven."

"Oh, Ray," Haven whispered. Ray looked up, loosening her grip on her dress. Tears pricked at the corners of Haven's eyes. "That sort of idea comes from Phoenix," she murmured, twining her fingers around the cloth that covered her knees. "I can tell you that much."

"Why is Ilonon like this, Haven?" Ray asked, burying her face in her knees again. "Why can't we just run away?"

"We could," Haven murmured. "And I agree with you, Ray. I'd like to get us all out of here. It's never safe. Never." Ray looked up through blurry eyes to see Haven shaking her head. "But the Blues are always listening." Haven let out a disgusted laugh, looking away. "The Blues are always listening," she repeated, pain in her expression.

"I think she means it even when they *aren't* listening."

"Mommy really thinks that hybrids should die?" Haven whispered. There was something like grief in her voice. Ray understood—it made her sick, too.

"Yeah," Ray answered. Her voice was a little too rough; she coughed. "Yeah," she whispered, not looking at Haven. "She thinks that hybrids should die."

"I—" Haven began. A sob caught in her throat, and Ray turned sharply to look at her. Laenyn began to stir in her sleep.

Haven seemed to be trying to laugh at herself, but the attempt was almost grotesque as her face contorted with tears.

"I see," Haven said, hiccuping. "I didn't know—I knew that Ilonon—" Haven broke off again, shaking her head and giving up the false smile. "But Mommy..." Her voice broke, and she put her face in her hands. "I thought Mommy was better than that."

Guilt welled up in Ray's chest. Floundering, she looked back and forth, hoping to find help, or a way to take it back. Haven didn't have to know! Finally, Ray scooted forward and pulled Haven into her lap, holding her tightly.

"There, there," Ray tried, feeling even more awkward than she sounded. Haven snorted.

"I can so tell that it's you, Ray," she laughed. It sounded almost like a sob. "You've never been any good with kids, have you?"

"Hell if I know," Ray said, grinning ruefully. Haven pressed her face into the crook of Ray's neck. "I can try to make you laugh by running into the wall or something, but I doubt Laenyn's nose would appreciate the gesture."

Haven laughed again, only hiccuping back a single sob. When she pulled back to look at Ray, the angled light highlighted the dark green ribbons that wound around Ray's arms in a crisscrossing pattern, making them catch her eye. They seemed almost to be a part of her skin. Ray looked back at Haven, who smiled with tear-stained eyes. Ray offered her the shoulder covering she wore on top of her dress.

"You can wipe your eyes on this," Ray said, half smiling as she lifted it up. "It didn't get too bloody, I think."

"Thanks," Haven murmured, leaning forward to wipe her eyes. When she pulled back again, her gaze was distant. "Just look at me, getting all worked up," she said. "I wish Marissa had taught me how to cook; it always made her feel better, didn't it?"

"Who?" Ray asked, leaning back on the balls of her feet. Haven's eyes snapped to focus on her, startled, and Ray tried to laugh it off. "I'd sure appreciate the food, in any case. I'm pretty hungry right now."

There was a pause. The light pouring through the window paper was blue.

"Right," Haven said, as the front door opened in the distance. "It's dinner time. I'd better get going."

"Will you be all right?" Ray asked, looking at her sidelong as she stood. Haven seemed distracted. "You look pretty unhappy."

Haven flashed a smile at her. "I think you need a nap, Ray," she said, rolling her eyes. "You're weirding me out by being this nice. I think sleepiness makes you sentimental."

"Wish it made Laenyn sentimental," Ray muttered, curling back against the wall. Haven had guessed right in one regard, at least; she felt exhausted. She yawned. "Instead, it just makes her grumpy and stubborn."

"If anyone's more stubborn, it's got to be you, Ray," Haven muttered. Continuing in a louder voice, she said, "Good night. I'll talk to you after dinner."

"Good night," Ray said, her eyes slipping closed.

"And thanks," Haven whispered. Ray was still smiling as she drifted off to sleep.

CHAPTER TWENTY-TWO

Laenyn watched Haven's guilty expression for a moment before waving it away with her hand. Hunger gnawed in her stomach, raw and obnoxious. It had been more than a full day since she'd last eaten; Haven and Wylwon had just returned from dinner.

"Don't bring me any food," Laenyn insisted. "It's my duty to purify myself with this fast, and you'd be beaten half to death for trying it."

"Wylwon—" Haven began.

"Received a lenient treatment, since they knew she'd taken it for a child who'd been too shaken up to eat," Laenyn said sharply, cursing Wylwon's kindness in her heart. "You'd be giving it to a woman who has been strictly forbidden by the Grand Council Woman *herself* from eating. That's a much greater offense. Perish the thought; don't let it so much as cross your mind this soon after a rebellion!"

Haven dangled her feet over the edge of the loft, not looking at Laenyn. Wylwon's eyes were clouded with regret, and Laenyn couldn't look at her.

"My dear," Wylwon began, then hesitated. "Haven, I know that I set a poor example for you, and for that I apologize. You must listen to your mother above anyone else."

"Even the Council?" Haven muttered, still not meeting their eyes. Laenyn winced.

"No," Laenyn said. "You know that's not what she meant, Haven. Why are you being so difficult tonight?"

"I—" Haven shook her head. "I don't want to talk about it."

"I am your mother," Laenyn said, twisting to dangle her own legs off the loft. "If you can't talk to me about it, to whom can you speak?"

Haven recoiled, a blush coming to her cheeks, and Ray turned over in her sleep. Laenyn felt cold realization strike at her heart, and she switched to English to hide the conversation from Wylwon.

"You want to talk to Ray," Laenyn said, embarrassed by the amount of hurt in her voice. Before Ray had come to her, Laenyn had trained away her emotions—as they made a resurgence, it was increasingly difficult to control them. "Why can't you talk to me about it?"

Haven just shook her head, her lower lip trembling. Laenyn turned away, looking at Wylwon.

"I speak small English," Wylwon offered, her eyebrows drawn together with self-consciousness as she tried to smile. "Maybe talk me?"

Haven shook her head again, still refusing to speak. The air in the house was quite cold; Laenyn wished that they had more than two outfits. Her other one had been left to soak in the bathroom hours ago, in the hopes of dredging out the bloodstains. She longed for a blanket, for food. It was Ray who longed for answers—why did it hurt so much that Haven didn't want to answer Laenyn?

I never cared before, Laenyn said, feeling Ray sleep and dream. *I could be hungry, or cold, or thirsty, and I just wouldn't care. I could blot it all out without a single thought. This is your curiosity, Ray, and I don't want it!*

Ray continued to sleep.

"Never mind," Laenyn said. "I won't ask. You should sleep now."

"I'm sorry, Mommy," Haven said, facing the wall without giving Laenyn so much as a glance. "I just—it's all muddled. I can't find any of the words."

"Good night," Laenyn replied. Haven's head sagged.

"Good night," Haven said, hurt burning in her voice—she sounded near tears.

"Good night, Haven!" Wylwon said, watching her hopefully. Haven just raised and dropped an exhausted hand before curling up on the pile of straw. Wylwon turned away, staring at the floor some nine or ten feet beneath them. "I'm sorry," Wylwon said. "I meant well."

Laenyn remembered crying in a corner as she hid all day, not allowed to go to the Main Hall, not allowed to eat. She remembered how it had felt for Wylwon to slip her an yraipyo; she remembered how ungrateful she'd been for that day of safety.

"I know," Laenyn said, her voice hushed and weary. "It's hard to understand rules when you're a child."

"Some rules must be disobeyed at times," Wylwon said, agony in her voice. "Orders that I can't follow. I'm not like you, daughter. I'm weak and all too human. It hurts to see her crying. It hurt then to see you crying. I never learned what disobedience was until I became a mother."

"The best way to protect her is obedience," Laenyn said, her voice firm and unyielding. Wylwon sighed, and Laenyn pushed forward. "Breaking rules results in punishments. To avoid punishments and attention and danger, we must obey."

"As I said," Wylwon said, coughing a little. "I—I don't know whether I was a good mother. I tried to do what I could. I got you out of my mother's house when you were three to try to raise you in safety."

"Your mother was a strong mother," Laenyn said. Wylwon

winced.

"You never had sisters, just like me," Wylwon said. "Males run in the family, I think. I'm sorry that I had to leave you alone so often."

Laenyn saw a pair of black eyes laughing in the darkness, and her hands tightened on the edge of the loft, her nail chipping against the wood.

"I will not bear children, Mother," Laenyn managed to say, a pain in her so deep that she couldn't tear it out. It was a weakness she'd never wanted. "We have Haven. I don't have to go Below."

"Of course," Wylwon said, a little bewildered. "I wasn't..."

"I think you need to get some sleep," Laenyn said. Wylwon hesitated, then pushed herself to her feet, dusting off her nakh—the simple cloth robe of a researcher, a profession so removed from the work of a Keshaan that a chasm seemed to stretch between them.

"Good night, Laenyn," she said. "Sleep well."

Laenyn said nothing as Wylwon walked behind her to climb down the ladder, and she didn't turn to watch her as she descended. Wylwon's feet padded quietly down the rungs, the soft sound loud in the silent house. Grief and guilt overtook Laenyn as Wylwon walked across the floor to reach her own loft. Wylwon's head was hanging, and—though she walked briskly enough that Laenyn wouldn't have been able to guess from sound alone—Wylwon's posture told all: she was exhausted, if not unhappy.

I always make a mess of things, Laenyn said to Ray, who kept sleeping. Wylwon climbed up to her own loft and curled up, shivering, to sleep. It was impossible to see very far in the darkness, but the shuddering breath and distinctive sound of the straw scraping against the floor were unmistakable.

Laenyn went over to her own bed, curling up beside Haven for warmth, and Haven rolled over, facing away from her. A twinge pierced Laenyn's heart, and she lay on her back, staring up into the darkness.

Why does she want to talk to you? Laenyn asked, startled by the bitterness in her own voice. *She hated you before. Why would she ever—I took her in!* Laenyn's eyes stung. *I never wanted to cry until you showed up!* Laenyn shouted at Ray's unmoving form. *I was strong.* She pulled back from Ray as Ray shifted in her sleep and continued in a more subdued tone. *What am I doing, telling you anything? You don't need to know me.*

Laenyn closed her eyes, willing her breaths to slow enough that she could feign sleep. Wylwon's snores from the other side of the house were comforting and familiar, but the night always brought the memories back. The eyes that watched her.

I don't deserve to be her mother, anyway, Laenyn said to herself. *I, I, I—Listen to me. I'm turning into you, Ray. When did this start?* Despair gripped her like a hand against her throat. *It was more than a year ago, now, I think.* The eyes that watched her filled her with terror and nausea. *I can't. I can't think. Not about that.*

The words she'd written on the floor the other night glowed before her, remaining even when she shut her eyes so tightly that they hurt. There was no way to claw them out of sight; the truth couldn't be destroyed.

What was it like to have sisters? Laenyn murmured. She shook her head slightly to dislodge the thought. *There's no point in asking. I'm a grown woman. I turned twenty this spring. It's too late for sisters; Mother is forty. What I should ask is why you were so outraged earlier.*

Ray continued to slumber, unmoved. Frustration built up in Laenyn's chest, making her dig her nails into her palms to ease the pressure.

It's all that I've ever known, Laenyn said. *Have you ever met a hybrid? They're dangerous! They bring misfortune to everyone in their lives! They break down the order of Ilonon; with hybrids, the whole system falls apart.* Laenyn suppressed a laugh, wild and desperate with disbelief. *But you'd like that, wouldn't you? You'd like for the whole system to come crashing down. It's all Jauge's fault, I think—* Laenyn froze, remembering Devolair's words from earlier in the day. *The honeyed lies of a... Lower?* Laenyn repeated the words in her mind, a chill creeping down her spine as she broke into a cold sweat.

Her mind reeled. They had checked every mind in the dinner hall; only Jauge took her meals separately, at her home in the woods. But Araya had been convinced of a plot to overthrow her —a plan from within the Council itself. Who knew enough about the Legend and its offshoots to twist the story?

"Oh, there's quite a different legend spread among the men, I'm told." Laenyn remembered Jauge's tone: she knew too much, too many things that she wasn't supposed to know. And she was *proud* of that. So proud of it that her arrogance had startled Laenyn. It had been one of a handful of conversations that she'd had with Jauge, all of them brief. The negotiations hadn't taken more than a few meetings.

Araya thought that the Primaries were going to side with the men and a new Ilonon would begin, with a new hierarchy, Laenyn turned the thought over in her mind, hardly daring to believe it, but everything rang true. *A hierarchy with White at the top.*

"The honeyed lies of a Lower," Devolair had said. Laenyn knew that voice too well: it was the voice that had slowly convinced Wylwon that she needed a lamp that would never run out, a wa-ter-proof cloth—inventions of Jauge's that would help at the lake. It was the same voice that had whispered in Laenyn's ear, telling her everything she wanted to hear, easing all of her pain with promises of a sleep without end...

The fierce, proud eyes burned in the darkness, watching her. Laenyn felt hounded on all sides, accused of cowardice and failing at all the duties that mattered most.

Jauge single-handedly overthrew the Council. Laenyn could see no other possibility; no one else had the means, motive, and craftiness to see such a plan through. *No one else has even the slightest chance to plan something like this, with the Blues listening at all hours.*

Laenyn wanted to write the words into the grain of the wood until her fingers were raw and her blood stained the words into the wood forever. She wanted to stop hiding; the guilt consumed her alive. It hadn't eased since she'd let Jauge experiment on her —if anything, it had intensified when Ray wasn't there to silence it.

As the walls closed in around her and Laenyn drowned in her own pit of despair and grief and guilt, she floundered for some sort of footing.

You should die! The specter in her heart spoke. You don't deserve to have a daughter and a kind mother. You appreciate nothing! You should give up and let Ray take over. Haven wants to talk to Ray more than she wants to talk to you, anyway. Just let go. That's all you deserve. A quiet, inglorious death in your sleep.

Laenyn squeezed her eyes shut. The words were too close to her heart, too true. There was nothing to grab hold of, nothing to save her from drowning in this abyss where she was utterly alone —*Help me!* Laenyn screamed, unable to move or speak. *Please, someone, help me!*

Ray's face swam in her vision, and she reached toward it, gasping for control of her lungs, which had quietly stopped filling with air.

Ray! Laenyn screamed. *Please, Ray! You have to save me!*

CHAPTER TWENTY-THREE

Ray, wake up!

Ray jumped, startled out of her dreams. The image of a woman with vivid, red curls and a sweet, cloying perfume standing outside the door burned in her mind for a moment before she found her surroundings. There was no light at all, but she felt straw beneath her, and Wylwon's snores seemed distant, making her guess that she was in her own loft. Listening closely for other sounds, she heard only Haven's slow, deep breaths at her side—the house was filled with silence. Gingerly, she lay back down on the straw, trying not to wake Haven.

What's wrong, Laenyn? Ray asked, trying to keep her heart from pounding. **I thought something was wrong! You scared me half to death!**

As Ray calmed down, she realized that Laenyn's walls were weak and hastily put up some of her own. As she did, she realized that relief was pouring from Laenyn, almost to the point of overwhelming them both.

I—I was bored, Laenyn said. *It's late at night, and everyone else is asleep.*

Oh, Ray said, relaxing a little. **That's all? Geez, Laenyn, don't scare me like that. I almost had a heart attack!**

I'm sorry, Laenyn said. *You can go back to sleep now, if you'd like.*

No, no, Ray yawned. **That's fine. Was there something in particular on your mind?**

I—I think that I'm ready to listen to you. About hybrids.

They're people, Laenyn. That's the entire problem, right there.

They aren't, Laenyn said. There was something desperate in her tone, something panicked. Ray glared at her, and she winced. *Make any other argument. Tell me anything but that. I'm trying to listen.*

Ray said nothing. Laenyn's anxiety swelled.

A hybrid is an aberration, something not meant by nature. Something that the Moons never intended.

Your proof being? Ray demanded.

Proof? Laenyn asked, perplexed. *Ask anyone in Ilonon, and they'll tell you the same.*

I'm asking you, Ray insisted. The straw mattress felt uncomfortable against her back; it had gotten cold enough that Haven had rolled over to cling to their side. **I want to know what sort of evidence you have backing your claim. Getting a lot of people to agree to something doesn't make it true, Laenyn.**

Laenyn sat back and thought for a long minute. Haven shuddered in her sleep, and Ray rolled over to drape her arm across Haven in the hopes of warming her. The night stretched on, and Ray began to drift off, thinking about home and the smell of rain in the air.

I can never truly know what the Moons intend, Laenyn said, her voice soft and mournful. *But the Council is appointed at their command, taking the purest of the Pure to govern the rest of us, and they have taught us that hybrids are a transgression in the Moons' sight.*

Is that the same Council whose leader went nuts and tried to kill the rest of them? Ray replied, sarcasm thick in her voice. Laenyn winced.

A new Council is being put in place as we speak, and I doubt that they will change their attitudes much.

But what if they did? Ray asked, the straw scratching at her arm as she pulled Haven closer. **What if they announced at breakfast that the Moons had told them that the previous Council was wrong, and that hybrids are totally okay?**

Laenyn was silent for a moment. *They wouldn't,* she said, very slowly. *They could never announce such a thing.*

Why?

They'd be overthrown, Laenyn said. *They'd be viewed as agents of the Lowest, the men and hybrids. They'd be stoned to death.*

Ray had the impression of white and blue flecks on her eyes and tried to blink the ghost lights away; the room was too dark to see anything tangible.

So even if the Moons floated down here themselves and told them to say it, they wouldn't? Ray prodded. Laenyn pulled back; Ray pursued her. **They'd be afraid for their lives, right?**

That's not— Laenyn began, her heart fluttering in Ray's chest. *Fine! How about this? If a hybrid is born, it will only have a weakened version of each power. Can they really be equal?*

But they'd have two powers, Ray insisted. **It's not a matter of higher and lower, Laenyn! You're all just people! There are bound to be personal differences, but who gets to judge who's really best?**

You can't be saying that Greens are the same as Blues! Laenyn laughed. Ray said nothing, only watching her, and Laenyn's smile fell. *You're not saying that we're all the same—we can't mix, Ray. We're like different species.*

If hybrids exist, that can't be true. You must be able to mix, or they wouldn't be around in the first place.

I—I don't want to believe you, Laenyn whispered fearfully. She had withdrawn so far that her back seemed to be pressed against a wall. *I don't want to think that you're right.*

What if Haven were a hybrid? Ray demanded. Laenyn gaped at her, her expression more horrified than it had been when staring into the torn out eyes of a skull.

How dare you! Haven pressed further against Ray's chest, trying to escape the cold. *They check everyone in the village; if they hadn't checked her, then they wouldn't have brought her to me. Haven is not a hybrid!*

But if she were? Ray pushed. **If she were every single Color all at once, would you still care about her as much as you do now?**

She's not! Laenyn shouted. *This is a stupid argument! Hybrids aren't like Haven—Haven is a good girl!*

So you've talked to hybrids? Ray scoffed. **What if she were, Laenyn? What would you do?**

If she were a hybrid, I'd be forced to kill her. Nausea lurked in her tone; she seemed ready to throw up.

You'd kill someone for being a hybrid?

I wouldn't have a choice. Laenyn buried their face in Haven's hair. *You don't understand. It wouldn't be my decision. I wouldn't have a choice.*

You always have a choice.

No. They would kill her anyway—they would tear her apart rather than a quick, painless death. They would kill Mother. They would kill me. If Haven were a hybrid and we'd harbored her, all of us would die unless I killed her myself.

Haven squirmed in Laenyn's too-tight embrace, and Laenyn eased her grip on her.

You don't understand, Ray.

That's right. I don't.

With that, Ray dropped the thickest walls that she'd yet managed to build between them, silencing any communication. Dimly, she felt Laenyn slam a frustrated fist against the wall, but then there was silence.

CHAPTER TWENTY-FOUR

Laenyn thought late into the night—Ray's words plagued her. The only conclusion she found was that the Primaries might not —*might* not—have power that was truly justified. Who made the rules? Who taught the Legend? The Uppers.

How do I know that the Moons decreed it? Laenyn asked herself. *I have only the word of the people who benefit the most from it!*

Laenyn paced back and forth in the closet. She knew the walls too well—they were a cage, thick enough to keep most sounds inside, bland enough that no one would have guessed that they were out of the ordinary. With long habit, Laenyn avoided catching her toe on the loose floorboard that hid their copy of the Rule Book. It might matter, someday—as though the rules were actually concrete, rather than made on the whim of an Upper.

Once, there had been a bit of clutter in the corners—many years ago, Wylwon had owned a few paltry possessions. But a Primary had seen them during an inspection and liked them enough to take them. Laenyn still remembered the termite-eaten stick that Wylwon had found for her—Laenyn had watched the woman order her assistant to burn it.

The day was dark beyond the window, and rain pattered on the roof. The air was cold and humid, like a pallid vapor had crept in to fill the house.

Laenyn paced, tapping her fingers against her thigh. Hunger clawed at her stomach with only water to nourish her, and her entire body seemed to jitter at its touch. She should exercise—she should train—but it was her conversation with Ray that lingered, seared into her ears. Ray had never felt the sting of the switch. She'd never had to witness a public execution. To her, it was abstract theory. Laenyn felt eyes on her—eyes that knew what was coming. Eyes that had walked knowingly into a proud and brave and undeserved death. Ray couldn't understand that.

Finally, Laenyn heard Haven at the front door, her bell jingling softly as she went up the stairs. Laenyn forced her feet to still and turned sharply to face the door as she waited for Haven. When Haven came in, she paused. Fear shone in her eyes.

"Hello, Mommy," she mumbled, quietly shutting the door. She pulled off her rain cloak, holding it in front of her, half hiding her face. "I'm sorry if you're mad at me. I promise I didn't bring you any food."

Laenyn's stomach growled, and embarrassment flooded her cheeks, making her cough.

"I'm not mad at you," Laenyn said, then groaned, trying to release the tension trapped in her shoulders. "I mean it, Haven. I'm mad at Ray."

"Why?" Haven asked, tilting her head to one side. Her red hair was vivid even in the dim room, a dark and lustrous red. No one in Ilonon had hair that hue.

"We've been arguing," Laenyn explained, looking away to resist the temptation of looking at Haven's footprints, a temptation that should have been long gone after years of practice.

"You never got mad at anyone before Ray got here," Haven mumbled, scuffing her feet. She lowered the cloak, setting it on the floor. "What are you arguing about?" she asked, her voice subdued but curious. Laenyn bit her lip.

"She doesn't understand anything," Laenyn said, though she knew that Ray had understood the goals of the Primaries too well, in a way that Laenyn had deliberately avoided seeing. "Did you know that she believes hybrids are people?"

Out of the corner of her eye, Laenyn saw Haven stiffen. As she turned, though, Haven's face was completely neutral, aside from her raised eyebrows.

"Really?" Haven asked, clearly skeptical. "I didn't know that anyone thought hybrids were *people*. All the villages that I've ever heard of just toss them right out as soon as they get caught."

"I know," Laenyn said, waving one hand while smoothing her braid with another. "I know! I don't know what to do. She doesn't understand."

"She's a stubborn one," Haven smiled. Laenyn turned away to look at the window, and Haven followed her gaze.

"It's going to be hard to know when to go to dinner," Haven murmured. "I hope that Wylwon leaves Lake Anonwe early, just in case the fumes come out in this weather."

"Mother knows how to handle herself," Laenyn said, looking at the gray window. "She's been studying the lake since before I was born."

They stood in a calm, comfortable silence for a long moment. Laenyn thought about Wylwon, and Ray's words the night before. She wondered what Wylwon would do if the Council ordered her to kill Laenyn or Haven. Laenyn would obey, but would Wylwon? Which was right? Her heart and head were at war.

"Are you still angry, Mommy?" Haven asked, snapping her out of her reverie. Laenyn shook her head.

"At least you understand," Laenyn said. She smiled at Haven, who gave her a wide smile in return. "You know that hybrids have to be driven out or killed."

"Of course," Haven said, her voice full of confidence. Her eyes seemed oddly bright, somehow—Laenyn dismissed the thought as Haven continued speaking. "I've seen what happens to hybrids," she said. "I understand exactly what you mean."

"Then I'm not mad," Laenyn said, the tension leaving her altogether. She patted Haven on the shoulder. "I'll even let you learn a few tricks about energy-magic from Ray, as long as you're both careful."

"Thanks, Mommy!" Haven said, smiling brightly. Laenyn was surprised by the little tears that pooled in the wrinkles at the corner of Haven's eyes as she grinned; she hadn't known how badly Haven wanted to be a Keshaan. "I'm going to take a nap to rest up, if that's okay."

"Go ahead," Laenyn said, watching her as she scurried off. She'd never seen anyone run as fast as Haven did. It was almost as though the girl could fly! Smiling proudly, Laenyn sank back against the wall. Midday of her second day of penance. At dusk tomorrow, she would have fresh blood on her hands.

Her smile fell away as the thought sank in. Outside, the rain turned into a frenzy, driving against the ground and roof so loudly that it sounded like the pounding of feet as they ran, or like a hand knocking at the door.

Ray stirred from her sleep. **Aren't you going to answer that?**

Answer what?

The door.

Laenyn leapt to her feet. The knocking at the door had become more insistent. Wylwon wouldn't knock. Fear swelled in her stomach.

Though she hesitated for a moment, once she got herself moving, she ran to the door. Her hand paused on the groove to slide it open. The wind howled and clattered outside, making the paper windows creak and groan.

"May I have the honor of knowing who it is that greets me?" Laenyn asked, swallowing to ease the knot in her throat.

"Jauge."

Jauge Haunobolon Kahn

CHAPTER TWENTY-FIVE

Laenyn slid the door open so suddenly that it squealed. Jauge was mostly dry, though she had a contraption at her side that dripped. As she made to lean it against the wall outside, Laenyn snatched it. The amount of fear that radiated from Laenyn as she took the opportunity to scan the street startled Ray, as did the amount of relief that came when Laenyn spotted no one.

What's going on? Ray asked. Though a part of her wanted to stay mad at Laenyn and keep up the walls of silence, a separate and more vocal part was curious.

"I'll lay this in the bathroom to dry," Laenyn said, making sure to keep her voice even, her face blank. Jauge looked at them with that piercing gaze—that gaze that knew more than it should. Ray felt Laenyn's nervousness increase tenfold looking into those cat-like eyes.

"Very well," Jauge said. Her tone was dry, but cordial. "May I come in?"

"Yes, of course," Laenyn said, making room and shutting the door behind Jauge.

Laenyn identified something critical in Jauge's gaze. Ray could see the disapproval, as well. The walls between them were too low; she wanted to examine Jauge without getting *all* of

Laenyn's interpretations. Ray built them up again carefully as Laenyn spoke.

"I'll be just a moment."

"Take your time," Jauge said. Before Laenyn turned to take what Ray recognized as an umbrella into the bathroom, she noticed that Jauge wasn't wearing a dress like the rest of the woman in Ilonon, and she had her own jacket, which Ray watched her remove as Laenyn turned.

What's the deal, here? What's Jauge doing here?

I don't know!

Ray looked around the bathroom as Laenyn leaned the umbrella against one corner. All that she saw was a pump and crank for getting out fresh water, and a quick glimpse of what she took to be a chamber pot. The concept was old-fashioned and unfamiliar to her, but she was able to recognize it through Laenyn's eyes. Laenyn must have used it while Ray was unconscious; Ray couldn't remember seeing inside it before.

"What is your business in Ilonon?" Laenyn asked Jauge, kneeling across from her. Jauge knelt, too—less formally. "Did you have some other task to inquire of me?"

"I wanted to see how you were doing after our meeting, Ray," Jauge said. Her eyes flashed, and Ray recoiled. "My, but you've become skilled at Yra."

"My name is Laenyn," Laenyn said, using English. "How did you find Haven's older sister, Jauge?"

"Laenyn?" Jauge repeated. She rapped the floorboards once with something like annoyance. "I told you—"

"Can you send me home?" Ray demanded, leaning forward as she took control of the body. "How did you bring—ahh!"

Ray cried out as her head seared with pain. It burned and pricked and boiled; if her skull split in half, it couldn't hurt any worse. Gritting her teeth, she tried to fight through it.

"Why did you—"

Stars burst before her eyes as the pain expanded, pressing

against every part of her skull. She could see and hear nothing—her body tensed, curling up of its own volition. Ray punched the ground with agony and frustration. She wanted answers, pain be damned!

"What's going on?" Jauge asked. "If this is some sort of show —"

"My name is Ray!" Ray spat out. The pain eased for the barest moment, and she managed to catch her breath. The rain drummed against the sill, spurring her onward. "My name is Ray, and I want to go home!"

Ray clutched her temples in her hands as everything resonated with the infernal pain—she imagined cracking her head open beneath the downpour, letting the rain soothe the charred folds of brain beneath the bone. Ray chewed her own tongue to help herself concentrate. She would do anything for the pain to stop.

Anything but never see home again. Anything but wake up every morning for the rest of her life prepared to kill or be killed. That wasn't a life she wanted. She wanted home, with her mother —who cooked when she was upset. With her sister—Meg, who loved to swim and collect trophies. With—Ray doubled over, grabbed her ears, and screamed into her knees as the memories floated upward bit by bit—only to shatter when they actually broke the surface. It was unbearable, it was excruciating—Ray writhed, incoherent and impotent with the sheer, torturous pain that exploded behind her eyes.

"Let her go!" Haven shouted. "Stop doing this to her!"

And it stopped. Ray was left panting on the floor. All she could think of was the absence of pain. Laenyn's voice, Haven's voice, Jauge's voice: they all meant nothing. Pressing her head against the cold, smooth floor, Ray breathed. Slowly, the words came into focus.

"I did hate her," Haven was saying. She sounded—wary? The emotion was hard to decipher. "How would you know that, though?"

"I know a lot of things," Jauge said gruffly. "I meant her no harm; I warned her that memories would only bring her grief."

Ray pushed herself to a kneeling position gradually, moving as though against a strong tide. The rain was still knocking against the walls and ceiling, unending. Breathing hard, Ray looked up at Jauge, not caring that there were tears in her eyes so thick that she could barely see.

"I want to go home!" Ray sobbed. "This place is terrible! I hate it. There's nothing good here. Why did you—" The pain flared for an instant, and she changed the subject, swallowing hard and choking on the frog in her throat. The world blurred before her. "All I want is to go home. Please, Jauge. I never did anything to you."

Ray blinked, sending the tears in hot streaks down her cheeks, and her eyes cleared. Jauge shook her head slowly.

"There is nothing I can do for you," Jauge said. "This was not what I intended. This is not at all what I intended."

Grief struck at Ray so sharply that it made her gasp. Her mother's face seemed to vanish, and her sister's name was swallowed by the sudden, aching void.

"So there's—there's no way?" Ray asked.

"It would be like falling into the sky," Jauge shrugged. "I can offer you nothing, and would offer you nothing even if I could provide you with some relief. Your mother, Wylwon, broke our contract. This experiment is a failure." Jauge got to her feet and dusted herself off. Laenyn seized control as Ray floundered in her lost hope.

"I know that it was you who tricked Araya," Laenyn said. Jauge paused, one arm in her coat. "You told her the male version of the Legend, the one in which the Primaries sided with White to overthrow Black."

Jauge pulled on the other sleeve of her coat, not speaking. Haven stared.

"Laenyn, I take it?" Jauge asked. Laenyn sat tall and proud, her chin resolute and high. "Keep the umbrella. I left a spare by the door."

"I want nothing of yours," Laenyn spat. "How did you, a Cotton White, persuade Araya to commit high treason? Even if you told her the Legend, how was that enough to convince her?"

"If you have no need of the umbrella, I'll leave it for Wylwon," Jauge said evenly. "Her work at Anonwe must be wearisome in such weather. Having ascertained that my experiment has failed, I think that it's time I leave."

Thunder rolled long and low across the sky. Jauge made for the door, but Haven stood in her way. Tears shone in her eyes as lightning made the window paper glow white, and the thunder crashed like a wave.

"Jauge," Haven said, giving her a pointed look. Ray watched, removed, as Laenyn ran to get in front of Jauge, where she could see both faces at once. Jauge's eyebrows were high with surprise; Haven and Jauge seemed to be having a conversation with their eyes alone.

"There is really nothing I can do," Jauge said at last, crossing her arms. "You know why that is better than anyone else in this room. Why not explain things and see how far that really gets you?"

Haven's eyes flashed, and Jauge laughed, tossing her head back—she sounded like a baying mule.

"Oh, I know why you won't," Jauge chuckled. Lightning flashed, and Ray noticed crisscrossing lines of slightly lighter skin on her arms, much like Laenyn's ribbons. They were almost imperceptible against her dark skin. "No need to tell me."

"And why won't you tell us why you brought her here?" Haven demanded. Ray felt Laenyn cringe, and sickness and horror alike clawed at their chest. Jauge's eyes pierced through them, seeing right into Laenyn's heart.

"Shall I tell her, Laenyn?" Jauge asked. Something of the laughter still caught in her voice, but her face contorted with something uninterpretable—a mixture of grief and rage and glee. "Shall I tell your daughter why you wanted to leave her? Why I took you away?"

"No!" Laenyn shouted, then looked at the door and covered her mouth. Jauge laughed again.

"You think you know guilt?" Jauge demanded. "You think you know shame? You know *nothing* of grief." Jauge began to laugh again, but Ray saw tears pooling in the crows feet that lined her eyes. It was a mockery of laughter—an awful, keening howl.

"Stop it, Jauge!" Haven shouted. Jauge's laughter cut off mid-guffaw, and her eyes narrowed to slits.

Jauge, leaning forward to speak directly into Haven's face, replied in a voice so low that the thunder drowned it out. Terror lit up in Haven's eyes. As the thunder died away, Laenyn opened her mouth to speak, but the door behind Haven slid open.

Wylwon's outline was lit by the white-hot streaks of lightning that raked across the sky above them. She shivered hard, robe and hair utterly sodden. Her hair had come entirely loose from its ponytail, and her chest heaved. As the lightning vanished, Wylwon blinked at them, taken aback. Glancing over her shoulder, she shut the door tightly behind her.

"What are you doing here, Jauge?" Wylwon asked, her voice low and full of pain. "Haven't you gone far enough with your—"

"I was just leaving," Jauge said, her voice crisp. Ray's heart felt as though it would break anew—the resurgence of longing to go home was so sudden and intense that she almost sobbed, but Laenyn shoved her down to silence her. Jauge glanced at them as though she'd heard. "I hope that you reap your harvest, Lady Laenyn," Jauge said, her tone like ice. "I will take my leave."

With that, she shoved Wylwon to one side, grabbing the dry umbrella that was propped against the wall beside the door, and stole out of the house.

No! Ray screamed. **You have to send me home! You have**

to do *something* to help me!

In the back of her mind, Ray heard laughter, and had the impression of despair beyond madness. It vanished, and the demon in her heart gave a cry so sharp it pierced through her—it had been struck dead. Ray sank into unconciousness. Laenyn gasped, feeling her chest.

"What just happened?" Wylwon demanded, shutting the door behind Jauge. "What was she doing here? She didn't...?" Wylwon touched Laenyn's temple gently, but Laenyn pushed her hand away.

"No," Laenyn said, looking at the floor. Jauge had left no footprints with her thick-soled shoes. "She declared the experiment a failure. Jauge has washed her hands of me."

"Good riddance," Wylwon said. Laenyn realized that Wylwon was trembling with the fierce cold.

"Let's get you out of these wet clothes," Laenyn said, her voice more gentle than before as she directed Wylwon to the bathroom. "We could call on your mentor's daughter to heat the bath."

"Of course we can't," Wylwon murmured, shaking like a leaf as Laenyn peeled away the sodden mess of cloth. "She's much too busy. You know that she became a midwife?"

"Did she?" Laenyn asked. Miss Maryl had been born the same year as Wylwon, and she had been the daughter of Miss Accen, Wylwon's instructor, but Laenyn knew little other than her name, and that she lived in the row of houses behind them. As one of the few Orange women that they knew personally, she'd been the first to come to mind. "I suppose that she would certainly make birthing easier. A hot tub to ease the pain..."

"And only the Lowers can get her," Wylwon smiled, wringing her hair out over the drain. It was a wild mess. "After all, no Primary would want to admit to having their attendant midwife be one of the lowest Secondaries."

Laenyn smiled slightly as she helped Wylwon into her second

dress, this time making sure that she had her rain cloak with her.

Haven watched the door with pensive eyes.

"I think it's time for dinner," she said. Laenyn remembered her hunger, so keen that it had devoured itself. Wylwon sighed as she wrung and stretched out her dripping clothes to dry.

"Very well, then," Wylwon said, turning to go. She laid one hand on Laenyn's shoulder and looked right in her eye, seemingly unable to speak. After a long moment, she squeezed Laenyn's shoulder. "Let's be off, then."

Wylwon Laenyn Emmerven

CHAPTER TWENTY-SIX

The rain continued, unabated in its downpour, as they left. Listening to the tides of thunder ricocheting in the sky above, Laenyn reached for Ray.

Do you think that the thunder is the judgment of the skies? Laenyn asked, feeling too alone in the wide house. She retreated to the closet. Ray slept fitfully, unresponsive. *Do the skies disapprove of the new Council?* Laenyn asked herself. *Or of Jauge's work?*

Help! Ray screamed. Laenyn jumped. **I'm drowning! I'm drowning! Pull me out of the water, please!**

Wake up! Laenyn replied. *It's just a nightmare!*

In their mindspace, Ray gasped for air, choking when she finally got it. Everything swam before her—her eyes burned as though they'd been submerged and exposed to chlorine, her lungs felt raw from lack of oxygen. Gasping and coughing and choking, Ray sobbed. The sound of the torrential, cascading rain seemed to swell.

Oh, God, Ray panted, clutching her knees. **What happened, Laenyn? What happened to me?**

You passed out when Jauge left. Laenyn drew back from her, hesitating before speaking again. *I—what were you dreaming about?*

Water, Ray replied. **Water on all sides, and two enormous hands holding me under. I screamed and screamed, but it only used up all my air, and I...** Ray shook her head. **I was going to die.**

It couldn't have been a nightmare, not like any nightmare that Ray had known before. The water had been bitter and mildly chlorinated, not like the black, mineral water at Anonwe or the clear water from the pump. Bit by bit, her heart and lungs were slowing. Laenyn was speaking; finally, after swallowing hard to ease the burning in her throat, Ray listened.

—and so I've decided that the rain must be an omen to that end.

I wasn't listening, Ray said flatly. **What I want to know is why Jauge wanted to experiment on you, and why you let her do it.**

Laenyn froze. *This isn't the time, Ray.*

It's never the right time, Ray said, leaning back against the wall. **When will it ever be the right time, Laenyn?**

Don't you remember what happened when you looked for answers before? Laenyn asked, her voice hesitant. Ray dug her fingers into their hair.

Yes, Ray said. She punched the ground. **Damn it! I just want to know what I'm doing here!**

You're being a thorn in my side, Laenyn said. The rain grew soft for a moment, and the thunder seemed distant. Laenyn touched her chest, where Ray felt a sharp pain. *You're making me question things.*

That's not what I... Ray began, then rethought her approach. There was no way back to Phoenix; Jauge must have burned all the bridges to get her here. Doing something about Ilonon, or to get them out of Ilonon, might be the only way to escape the atrocities that she'd seen and heard about. Fighting down the agony in her heart that cried for home and family, Ray closed her eyes. **What am I making you question?**

The Primaries, Laenyn whispered. There was a note of fear in her voice. *It's dangerous to have these kind of thoughts, Ray, but I can't ignore them when you won't just accept them. I never thought to question **why** the Primaries told us the Legend.*

Good, Ray said. **Have you been thinking about hybrids, too?**

I'm going to be a full-fledged Keshaan tomorrow night, Laenyn whispered. *Keshaan are supposed to enforce Ilonon's laws. How can I possibly start questioning them now, Ray? Especially—especially about the hybrids.*

What do you mean, especially? Ray asked, a creeping horror rising in her chest. A part of her wasn't sure that she wanted to hear the answer to the question.

Well, Keshaan play a different role than Keshaan apprentices. Laenyn's voice was evasive, but Ray pressed her with a hard stare, and she continued. *Keshaan don't have to perform executions. They deal more in beatings. That's why they're having the apprentices execute the previous Council members. It's going to be our last time being forced to—*

No. Ray's voice was aghast—she couldn't process the thought. **You—you were ordered to kill—** Bile rose in her throat. The scent of blood seemed to hang in the air; Ray rubbed her hands together unconsciously. **You didn't!**

I— Laenyn backpedaled. *I've— Don't look at me like that!*

They were making you *kill* people, and you stayed? Ray gasped.

The enemies of Ilonon aren't people! Laenyn shouted, guilt and grief in her voice. *I did nothing to violate any law—I only followed my orders!*

That's it, Laenyn. Ray snapped, her voice tight and furious. **Who are the enemies of Ilonon?**

Those who break the law, those who create unrest, and—and those who are hybrids. Those are the enemies of Ilonon.

Why did you stay?

I stayed because of my obligations, Laenyn whispered. Tears pricked their eyes. *To my mother, daughter, and village.*

Ray found herself pacing, too horrified to speak. After a long, long moment, she swallowed.

We need to escape, she said. **You may have been able to handle this, but I can't, Laenyn. I *can't.***

There's no way out! Laenyn cried, her voice rich with agony. *There are beasts in the forest, and the fog at Anonwe is toxic! To lose a Keshaan would be such a great affront, especially so soon after a rebellion, that they'd have to make an example of us. You don't understand what sort of dangers there are in Ilonon!*

Ray sank against the wall, her head spinning. The door to the closet opened as Haven walked in, dripping wet. Her rain cloak was so drenched that it left a trail of water behind her.

"Hi," she said, shivering. Her right hand clutched her left arm so tightly that it was turning white. "Are you doing okay?"

"What happened?" Ray asked, eager to stop thinking about being trapped in hell. Haven winced and turned away, her sodden hair falling to hide her face.

"Oh, nothing, really," Haven said, shrugging. "It's just a little cut. I wanted to say good night, then go right to bed. It's been kind of a long day."

"A cut?" Ray said. Haven nodded. "Come on, Haven. You can tell me what happened."

"It's nothing," Haven repeated, squeezing it more tightly. "I just wanted to see if you were okay before going to sleep. The way you..." Haven licked her lips and shook her head. "Earlier, when your head started to hurt—I guess I got scared. But Mommy would probably know what happened."

One lash of the rod, Laenyn supplied. *Probably for stuttering. They hate it when she stutters. It's all they need to remember she's a foreigner.*

"You're right," Ray sighed. The rain rattled the window

panes, suddenly picking up again. A low rumble of thunder boomed in the distance. "I guess the storm is looping back around."

"Yeah," Haven said, rolling her eyes. "It's like a thick mist out there. I guess the drops are getting bigger now. Maybe that means that it's going to end soon."

Ray shrugged. Haven had already had a rough day; she didn't want to worry her with their conversation. Ray needed more time to think, but what she wanted was a distraction.

"Are you okay?" Haven asked, touching Ray's leg with her injured hand. Ray tried to smile to dispel the worry clouding her eyes, but Haven didn't smile back. After a long moment, she nodded. "You look kind of like you don't want to talk about it. I—I can stay up a little longer, I guess." She forced a smile, but her grip on her arm was starting to make Ray worry. She could cut off the blood flow through that arm, and that could really do some damage. "Mommy did promise that she'd let you teach me a few energy-magic tricks."

You did?

It seems like a lifetime ago, but I did. Laenyn said. *I don't know what I was thinking. I guess I was just so relieved... But there's nothing to be done now. I can't go back on a promise.*

"Seems so," Ray said, stretching to reach for her staff. "I'll just show you how to make fire. It's about the simplest to try, and Laenyn and I can put them out right away, so it's also the least dangerous. Wanna give it a go?"

"Sure!"

The rain drummed against the walls, and thunder boomed and crackled soon after lightning lit the window beside them, casting Haven's face in sharp relief. When it cleared, Ray realized how dark the room had gotten.

"Okay, so I'm going to hold up the staff," Ray said, doing so as she watched Haven. "Then I just need to think about—about something that makes me angry. If I can focus that energy on lighting up the staff, presto, it should glow just the way I want it to. Sound good?"

"Sounds pretty simple, if you just have to get mad at it," Haven said. "Okay. I'm ready."

Ray squinted at the staff through the dim air, trying to block out the storm. She reached deep inside herself, looking for the anger that had fueled so much of her magic before. No matter what she tried, though, nothing worked—the unnatural anger was gone. Feeling a little awkward, she turned to Laenyn.

A little help?

I don't want to make you mad any more, Laenyn said. *We've argued more than enough.*

Ray thought back on their arguments, and realized that she'd been focusing on the wrong things—things that would have provoked the old anger, but nothing to fan the more recent flames. So she thought about how they couldn't escape—how she couldn't keep people from getting hurt—how many people had died and how she could do nothing to save them, and her staff burst into brilliant, dark green flames that licked her hands without hurting her. Haven gasped.

"Then you have to slowly reabsorb the energy," Ray said, trying to keep the fire going as she spoke. "If you go too fast, it's going to hurt like hell. If you lose any of it, you're going to age unless you sleep it off right away. Got it?"

Haven's face was lit with green as she nodded, the shadows stark and flickering as Ray started to take the energy back into herself. Finally, they were submerged in darkness once again. Ray blinked, trying to erase the shadow that the flames had left on her eyes, then rolled Haven the staff.

"Your turn," Ray said, smiling. Somehow, turning the anger into flames had made her a little less ill at ease; it had been satisfying.

Haven picked up the staff and settled down on the floor—she bit her lip and pushed her hair back, out of the way of potential flames. She stared at the staff, building focus. Ray was startled at the fury that suddenly swept across Haven's face as she brandished the staff, making it burst into brilliant flames.

Ray gawked. The flames that reflected in Haven's horrified eyes were a mixture of almost every Color that Ray had learned—half of the flame was blue, but before Ray could make out the rest of them, Haven had thrown the staff away, sending it slamming against the wall beside Ray. It bounced and rolled back to Haven's feet—she was standing.

No. Laenyn breathed. Ray didn't move, staring with shock at the staff. Things clicked into place so quickly that Ray could bare-ly breathe. Haven had let go of her arm; as white lightning lit up the window, Ray realized that her blood was a kaleidoscope of colors.

"No," Haven whispered, her eyes brimming with tears. "Not again. Not again!"

Those colors—

Haven is a hybrid.

Haven Emmerven

CHAPTER TWENTY-SEVEN

No! Laenyn screamed. Haven backed toward the door, hand rising to her throat. She tore off her bell and dashed it against the wall, then turned and fled, leaving footprints that swirled chaotically in her wake. *Not my daughter! Not my daughter!*

Ray was already on her feet and giving chase. Wylwon grabbed at her arm as she ran toward the open front door, saying something in an urgent voice that was drowned out by the blood rushing in Ray's ears. Ray shook her arm off, but Haven had a head start, and Ray couldn't see through the rain, which was so cold and heavy that it knocked the wind from her lungs.

This is impossible! Laenyn screamed. It was distant—the fear roiling in Ray's belly was so fierce that she almost vomited.

Hybrids were supposed to be killed. If Haven were caught—Ray's heart pounded so hard that she was afraid it would burst; she felt dizzy and ill.

Haven is a good girl! She can't—she can't be a hybrid!

Ray peered through the darkness, so thick and wet that her eyelids were heavy and blurred with raindrops. Lightning rushed across the sky, splitting it in half, and a thousand rainbows arced across the drops clustered in her eyelashes; Haven's footprints had been washed away. Ray was sinking into the mud.

She's trying to escape, Ray guessed, turning toward the forest. Running blindly through the slick mud, Ray could barely understand what she was seeing when the lightning raced across the sky again. The ground seemed to ripple, too wet to just shake. An earsplitting cry that Ray knew would haunt her nightmares for the rest of her life—a monster whose three eyes glowed in the lightless sky.

"No!" Ray screamed, trying to run faster. She slipped in the mud and hit the ground hard. The thunder drowned out her cry, and lightning struck a tree in the forest, lighting the scene from behind. The Haubonalyr had white scales—and a little, green spot that dangled, speared, from a scythe-like spike on its tail. Haven. It had Haven. It brought her to its mouth and tore at her cloak, spitting the rest out and wiping it off on a tree near the field. Ray watched it, unable to even scream through the horror.

Laenyn screamed, though. Grief and regret and horror and guilt so thick and overwhelming that it gnawed all the way to Ray's numb, shocked core—a scream that was the keenest expression of emotion that Ray had ever heard.

Not Haven! Laenyn cried out, sobbing so hard that Ray doubled over to vomit bile into the mud. They'd eaten nothing for more than a day, but she kept gagging. *I don't care if she's a hybrid! You can't take my daughter from me! You can't take Haven from me!*

Laenyn snatched control of their body. She didn't have her staff; she didn't care. Women were watching her from the windows, and she didn't care. She'd been ordered to stay in her house like a good little girl, and she didn't fucking care. With a howl of rage so intense it almost tore her apart, Laenyn ran at the Haubonalyr. She had nothing more than her bare hands and her hatred.

Give me back my daughter!

Laenyn swung one arm upward, yanking the energy from the Haubonalyr, aging it so rapidly that she could see its scales rotting. High above them, Laenyn gripped the glittering energy that had sustained the beast. In the bright relief of its light, Laenyn saw that the ground was littered with other corpses, and that other Keshaan were fighting. The Haubonalyr's life-energy coursed through her body; every synapse shuddered and burned, unable to contain it, unable to channel it and survive. The other Keshaan began to sink to their knees, watching the light—recognizing her green.

Laenyn's body was flooded with fire, hunting for an outlet—there were trees behind the Haubonalyr. They would do; trees could die. Ray helped her move the dark, crackling energy through the air like a lightning bolt. Laenyn thrust the energy toward the forest, and half a dozen trees shrank to nothing as a low, crackling fire consumed the new saplings and the moldering Haubonalyr. Then the light vanished, and the rank stench of burnt flesh swept across the village. Laenyn staggered forward, trying to reach for Haven, tears burning in her eyes, her voice ragged and pained.

"Please," she begged, stumbling and barely catching herself. "I have to—"

Ray caught their body as Laenyn sank, her presence vanishing utterly. Ray fell to her knees in the rain, staring through her fingers at the blood that ran in the soil beneath her.

Laenyn, wait. Ray said, numb. **Wait, wait. We finally agree. We have to go get Haven.**

Nothing but silence answered her.

Laenyn, please! Ray shouted, curling inward. **Please, Laenyn! I can't face all of this alone!**

There was no answer, no presence. Laenyn was gone.

Swaying, Ray pushed herself to her feet. Her legs ran of their own accord, drawing her toward Haven. She tripped twice over body parts, but she didn't dare look closely at them. Finally, Ray reached the tree against which she'd seen the Haubonalyr throw Haven. She sank down beside Haven's crumpled form, finally feeling the rain that had soaked so thoroughly into her.

Lightning tore across the sky, illuminating Haven's blood-soaked cloak. The rainbow blood was the same that Ray had seen earlier, unmistakable.

"No," Ray whispered, touching the cloak. "Haven..." Tears were hot on her icy cheeks. There was something thick and yellowish clinging to the place where the Haubonalyr's spike had pierced Haven. It burned to the touch, and Ray scrubbed her hand in the mud.

Haven had been eaten alive.

CHAPTER TWENTY-EIGHT

The sun shone overhead, bright and hot. Ray looked around, dazed. She found herself slumped over the edge of the pool. Meg knelt beside her, offering her a hand with a sad expression.

"It's time that you come inside," she said softly. "It's too hot out here."

"Where's Haven?" Ray asked, her voice younger than she expected—she was in her own body again, using her own voice. Meg pointed to the pool, and through the heat haze, Ray made out Haven kicking around the shallow end, hair bright as fire. Leaping toward her, Ray sunk under the water again.

The water was cold enough to stun her, and the chlorine was salty as blood in her mouth. Or maybe they were tears.

Tears. Ray blinked in the torrential downpour, tears stinging in her eyes as she clutched Haven's cloak and wailed through the thunder. She'd been too late, too late.

Haven's in Phoenix, Ray thought, the words fitting together strangely. Everything seemed to be disintegrating around the edges, and Ray was falling upward through the storm. **Maybe— maybe I can follow her.**

The rain halted, floating before her eyes. Ray felt spun head over heels as the water poured into the pool, surrounding her on all sides. She surfaced, gasping for breath, and the pool seemed to stretch on for ages—the sun was blindingly bright.

"Haven!" Ray called, squinting through the light. Her heart was in her throat, and water filled her mouth, making it hard to breathe. "Haven!" Ray screamed, spitting out the water. "Where are you?"

A hand grabbed her foot and pulled her under again. Ray clapped her hands over her mouth, trying to hold her breath even as it burned and burned, her eyes shut tightly against the chlorine. The nightmare came back to her as her eyes stung and her lungs screamed for air and everything turned into a haze of red and black until the hand released her and the tide sent her spinning through the cold—finally, she gasped, and the world righted itself.

The air was freezing and thick with mist. Ray opened her eyes, breathing hard; she was facing the battleground, still clutching Haven's cloak to her chest. It was too dark to see clearly, but Ray could dimly make out the mangled corpses that she'd tripped over to get this far.

Laenyn? Ray sobbed. There was no sound—she had their entire mind to herself. Remembering Dayan putting herself out like a light to fight the first Haubonalyr, Ray felt sick to her stomach. **This can't be real,** Ray said, shutting her eyes. She had all the time in the world to think things over, all the quiet that she needed—she wanted noise. The mist settled into her dress, and Haven's cloak was crusty with dried blood and venom. **None of this was real!** Ray shouted into their empty mind. **Go on and prove me wrong, Laenyn! Just when I was getting close to Haven—just when I could have agreed with you—Ilonon can't be real!**

The pain in her chest and throat was overwhelming; she'd sobbed herself dry, but she continued choking on tears and bile as she buried her face into the scratchy fabric of Haven's bloody cloak.

This isn't real! Ray screamed. **It's got to be a nightmare!**

The mist swelled. When Ray opened her eyes again, she was standing in the shallow end of the pool, looking down at Haven. Haven didn't meet her eyes, still splashing around in the hazy heat. Nothing was distinct. Somehow she was in a swimsuit—she thought it had been red before, but when she looked down again, all that she could see was Laenyn's green.

"It's time to come inside, Ray!" Meg called, and Ray turned to see her standing on the shore, far away, cupping her hands around her mouth.

"I'll bring Haven!" Ray called back, turning to grab her, but Haven wasn't there. The pool's horizon was farther than she could see. Ray splashed back and forth. The panic surfacing in her chest made the water ripple.

"She's already inside!" Meg shouted. Ray turned, and the shore—the steps—were much closer, and the water seemed to be shallower. Meg was holding out her hand, and Ray could see their mother inside, a sad smile the only part of her face not obscured by the heat haze. "Come on! Mom cooked lunch for us!"

Ray's stomach growled. It felt like it had been years since she'd eaten anything that wasn't cold, and the chill in the water was making her toes and fingers go numb. She moved toward Meg. Though she had barely moved, her foot connected with the bottommost step, and she found herself looking up at Meg's sorrow-filled expression.

"It was all a nightmare?" Ray asked, her voice childish and scared. All the anger that had gnawed at her in the summer heat was long gone. She wanted no more of the pool, no more of the cold. Meg's eyes seemed misty with tears.

"Don't pay it any mind," Meg whispered, taking Ray's hand. Meg's hand was so hot that Ray felt scorched by the touch and gasped. When Ray tried to pull back, the heat eased, and Meg shook her head. "No, Ray. You belong here, with us."

"Here?" Ray asked. "In Phoenix?"

"Yeah," Meg nodded, swallowing to loosen her voice. Something about her tone made Ray nervous; somehow she was already on the top step, ready to get out into the heat. As she raised her foot, she heard a door slam.

"No, Meg!" Haven's voice called, and Ray caught a glimpse of Haven running at her from the corner of her eye. Meg released Ray to turn and look back at Haven; Haven's eyes were full of tears. "She still—not yet!" Haven cried. "We can't take her yet!"

"I thought you hated her?" Meg asked, her voice warped by the sound of the wind, and though Ray felt nothing, the water of the pool seemed colder and more real than before. Haven was shaking her head.

"She's not the same Ray!" Haven said desperately. "There was a—no!"

Ray's feet were so cold that the rest of her was starting to shake. Holding herself against the sudden wind driving her away from warmth and home, Ray stretched to take that final step. Haven ran at her, arms first, driving her backward and pushing her under the water.

Ray gasped, jumping at the startlingly cold bite of the water. Blinking at the light around her, Ray thought for a moment that she was underwater. Finally, she realized that someone was stooping over her, calling a name that she recognized.

"Lady Laenyn!" the woman called, shaking her. Ray blinked again to clear the tears and mist from her eyes. The sky was overcast and the air was cold, but there was enough light to see. Ray blinked up at the woman above her, who had bright, blue eyes and sandy blonde hair. Her relieved smile was the most unfamiliar thing in her face.

"What?" Ray said. Where had Meg and Haven gone? Reality began to sink in as she felt Haven's cloak in her hands.

"Oh, thank the stars," the woman said. Ray looked down at the rest of her body as the woman sat back, and Ray noticed her swollen, pregnant belly, as well as the pink, cotton dress that

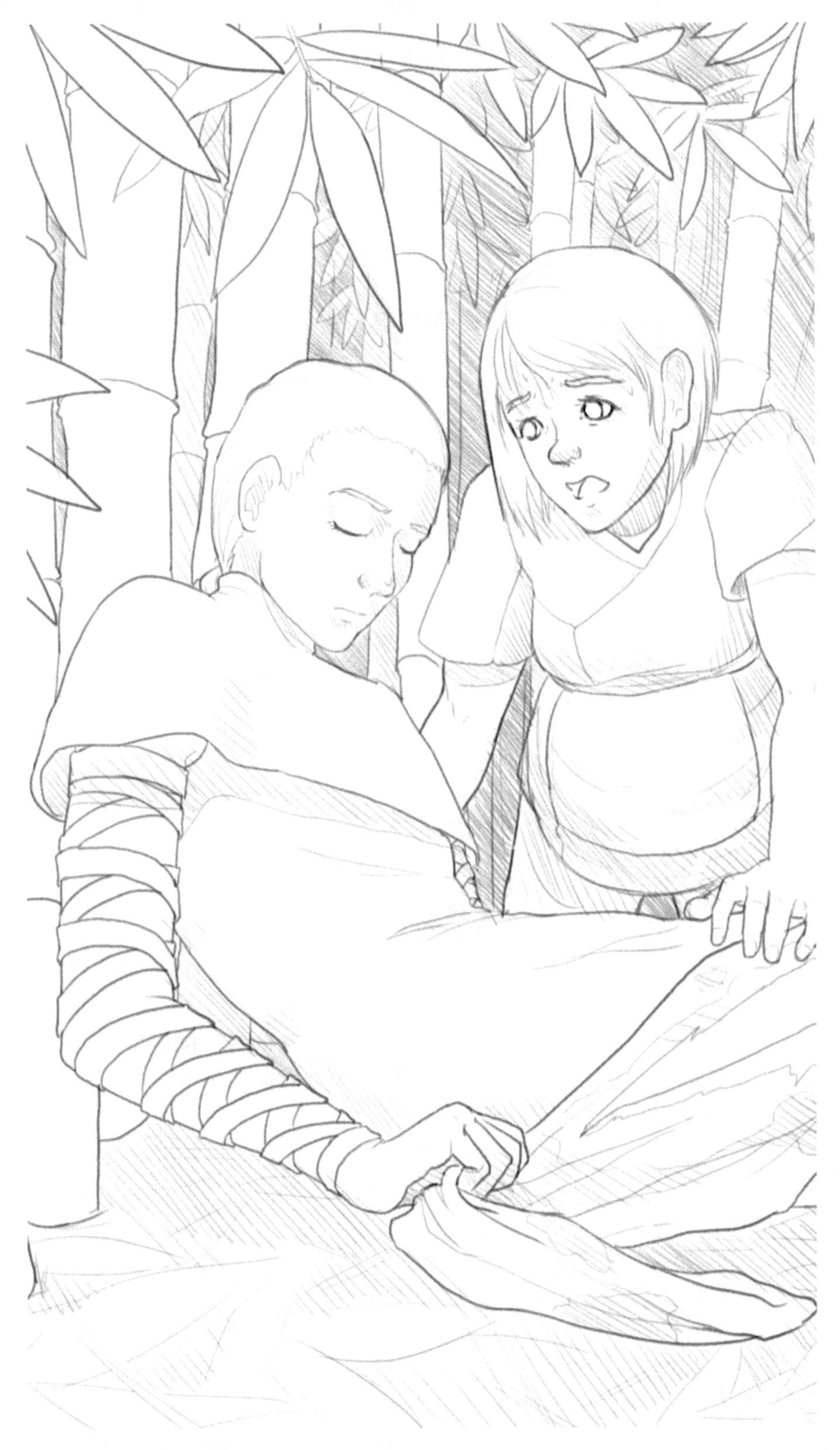

stretched taut across it. "You're the first live one I've found—all the rest dragged themselves home. What made you stay?"

Ray dug her fingers into Haven's cloak, barely suppressing the urge to vomit up stomach acid again. Remembering that Haven was dead made her heart ache.

"My daughter," Ray whispered, not sure why the word *daughter* came so much more readily than *sister* to her lips. Tears budded in her eyes. "I was too late."

The woman reached out to take her hand, then hesitated.

"She was lucky to have a mother who cared so deeply for her," the woman said, responding in English. Ray realized that she'd been using English since she'd seen Meg again. Pinks had the gift of language—useless in Ilonon, but so comforting then that Ray's chest hurt. Unable to speak, Ray nodded, and the woman unconsciously touched her own stomach as she continued in a hushed, pained tone. "I am so sorry for your loss."

Ray didn't want to face it. Gagging again, she shut her eyes against the sunless daylight.

I want to go home! Ray shouted, wanting Laenyn to respond and choking on tears when she didn't. **None of this is real!**

"My lady?" the woman asked, touching Ray's shoulder. Vertigo pinned Ray to the sandy sky, dangling far above the misty ground. Nausea roiled around Ray's stomach. The world around her was too detailed, too tangible, too cold—she wanted to go back to Phoenix.

"What's your name?" Ray asked, trying to ground herself.

"Syrian Monyn," she answered. "Do you need assistance returning home, my lady?"

Before Ray could speak, she heard a high, cold voice somewhere behind Syrian, a voice that made Syrian shrink back and out of the way immediately.

"Step aside, filth!" the youthful voice growled. As Syrian ducked aside, Ray saw a little girl dressed entirely in black silk that shone clean in the misty light. Her hair hung past her waist, perfectly straight, black, and glossy; her coal-like eyes were the eyes of a corpse, sunken into her too-pale, ashen skin. A child's hand lay at her feet—the little girl kicked it aside without giving it a second glance. Ray shrank beneath her gaze.

"Please pardon me, Lady Octavia," Syrian said, her voice high with terror. "I will return to my duties."

"Who have you found?" Octavia demanded, staring down at Ray with a snarling lip—Ray saw fangs and swallowed. "A Lower. What good is a Lower to us?" Octavia snapped, glaring at Syrian with such hatred that Ray recoiled. "You've found no more survivors?"

"N-no," Syrian breathed, not able to look at Octavia's eyes. She sank into a low bow, resting her forehead on the ground. Her thick, muscled arms stretched out in obeisance before her. "There are only body parts. We have assembled many, but it is difficult to identify—"

"Excuses!" Octavia snarled, her voice little more than a wolf's growl. Her face shifted before Ray's eyes, and her fangs extended past her lips. "A Lower has no place as a Keshaan."

"She saved us," Syrian said, snapping upright. Ray was surprised by the fierce light in her eyes.

"Are you talking back to me?" Octavia asked. Syrian stiffened, but Ray saw her jut out her jaw the slightest degree. Octavia dropped down onto all fours, her arms growing longer, and Syrian held her breath. "I asked you a question, *filth*."

Syrian refused to speak, but didn't duck her head or look away—her eyes smoldered as they met Octavia's.

"You!" Octavia said, rounding on Ray. "Put her to death for her insolence!"

"My baby has done nothing—"

"We need no more of your kind in Ilonon," Octavia sneered.

"I won't," Ray said. Syrian looked at her, startled. "You can't make me kill her."

"I can and will," Octavia replied. "If you object, your mother will join you in your fast."

Wylwon's agonized cry came back to Ray: 'Just once—just *once*—I wish that I could protect you, instead.'

We can run, Ray thought. **We don't need Ilonon.**

"No," Ray said. She looked at Syrian, whose expression was inscrutable without Laenyn to interpret it. Ray remembered English. "Syrian, you have to run."

"Disobedience will not be tolerated," Octavia hissed, hackles rising. Only barely human, her eyes seemed to twist within her melting skull. Her eyes were on Ray; Syrian looked at the forest, then back to Ray.

"Then I guess you'll have to kill me," Ray taunted, drawing attention away from Syrian as she started to rise. Octavia didn't fall for the ruse—her head snapped around, and she brought a heavy paw down on Syrian's leg, pinning her to the ground. Ray's head swam.

"No," Ray heard herself say. "I won't kill her. I won't kill."

"Then you chose the wrong profession," Octavia growled, narrowing her eyes on Ray once again. The hairs on her arms stood on end, getting thicker and sharper, and her mouth transformed into a muzzle, dripping with saliva and full of fangs that were sharp enough to make Ray's blood run cold.

Octavia morphed into a wolf with curved fangs longer than the breadth of Ray's hand, standing at least five feet tall at the shoulder. Ray breathed hard, shoving herself back against the bark without losing her grip on Haven's cloak. Octavia snarled, stepping backward onto Syrian's legs. Distantly, Ray heard something crack, and Syrian screamed. But Ray's gaze was fixed on Octavia's coal-black eyes, full of madness.

Octavia leapt, and Ray sank.

Octavia Thyn

CHAPTER TWENTY-NINE

Meg pulled Ray, sputtering, out of the pool and into the warmth. The sun shone above her, bright enough to make her eyes hurt. Ray gasped for air, even though she was totally dry— Meg looked at the water with regret.

"You belong here, with us," Meg said, helping Ray to her feet. Even though she was shaking, Ray seemed to weigh nothing, and she stood without trouble. Meg inclined her head toward the house. "Come on."

"Where's Haven?" Ray demanded, looking around. Meg's eyes shone with pain, and Ray caught sight of Haven wandering around the shallow end, looking lost.

"She wanted to keep swimming," Meg murmured. "It's going to get stormy soon. It's not going to be an easy swim."

"Should I—" Ray began, but Meg shook her head. Ray remembered that Meg was four or five years older than her, and Meg suddenly seemed taller as she reached down to grab Ray's shoulders and stare into her eyes.

"Haven will come in when she's ready," Meg insisted, looking intently into Ray's eyes. "You had a nightmare. Don't worry about it. You don't have to think about any of it any more. We have plenty of food in the house; I know that you must be hungry after your swim."

"I—but Haven—" Ray stumbled, trying to look back as the house door swung shut behind her.

"She'll be in later," Meg said. "Come on. Dad's out with—well, you know who he's out with. But Mom made us lunch. It's all your favorites."

"Don't drip on the hardwood floors, now," Ray's mother said, a smile in her voice that didn't appear on her face. Ray didn't recognize her eyes. "You girls must be cold. Have some towels and eat up."

Ray sat at the wooden table, suddenly swathed in a thick, warm towel. Food kept appearing before her—grilled cheese, ramen, pizza—and there was always enough to drink. She felt drugged; Ilonon began to fade with a few bites of the painfully nostalgic foods that didn't fill her any other way. More bread, more sides, more food—it made her forget the hunger, the pain.

Was it all a bad dream? Ray asked herself, lying back on her bed as she stared at the ceiling and listened to Haven splash around in the dark backyard. Something in her heart whispered: Good is more real than evil. It was nothing more than a bad dream; go on and let it go. Aren't you happier here? Why would you want to go back *there*?

So during the day she lived a dreamlike life, where there was always enough and no one got punished for things that weren't their fault.

And at night, she dreamt of Wylwon's tear-stained face begging her to wake up.

Color Chart

Black: Transformation

Can alter any aspect of their bodies at will with practice.

Blue: Mind-reading and -control

Can access surface thoughts, implant thoughts, and, with practice or talent, can control specific areas of the brain.

Red: Pattern and data crunching; intelligence

Can mentally identify complex patterns and solve high level equations.

Yellow: Energy

Needs only an hour of sleep per night.

Gray: Plant growth

Can grow a seedling to full height in a day.

Brown: Weather control

Can control the water content and temperature of the air within thirty yards of them; careful manipulation of these elements moves and creates clouds, wind, etc. In groups, they can extend their reach to low-hanging clouds.

Purple: Psychokinesis

Can move up to 200 pounds with their mind.

Green: Health

Never become sick; can survive on one meal every three days (not comfortably).

Orange: Fire

Can create and control flames up to the size of a small building.

Pink: Languages

Can speak any language after gathering enough of the syntax.

White: Increased sensory control

Can adjust pupils at will; can shut out or amplify what they hear at will.

Artist Galleries

Susan Lau: Character Concept Art, Character Scenes
   shatteredearth.net

Jeff Miller: 3D Haubonalyr Model
   jeff3dsculpt.daportfolio.com

Gail Lynn Sapitan: Cover, Setting Concept Art
   bluer-skies.net

Katinka and Tamara Thorondor: Action Scene
   cobravenom.deviantart.com
   ilenora.deviantart.com

Herwin Wielink: Map
   fantasy-maps.com